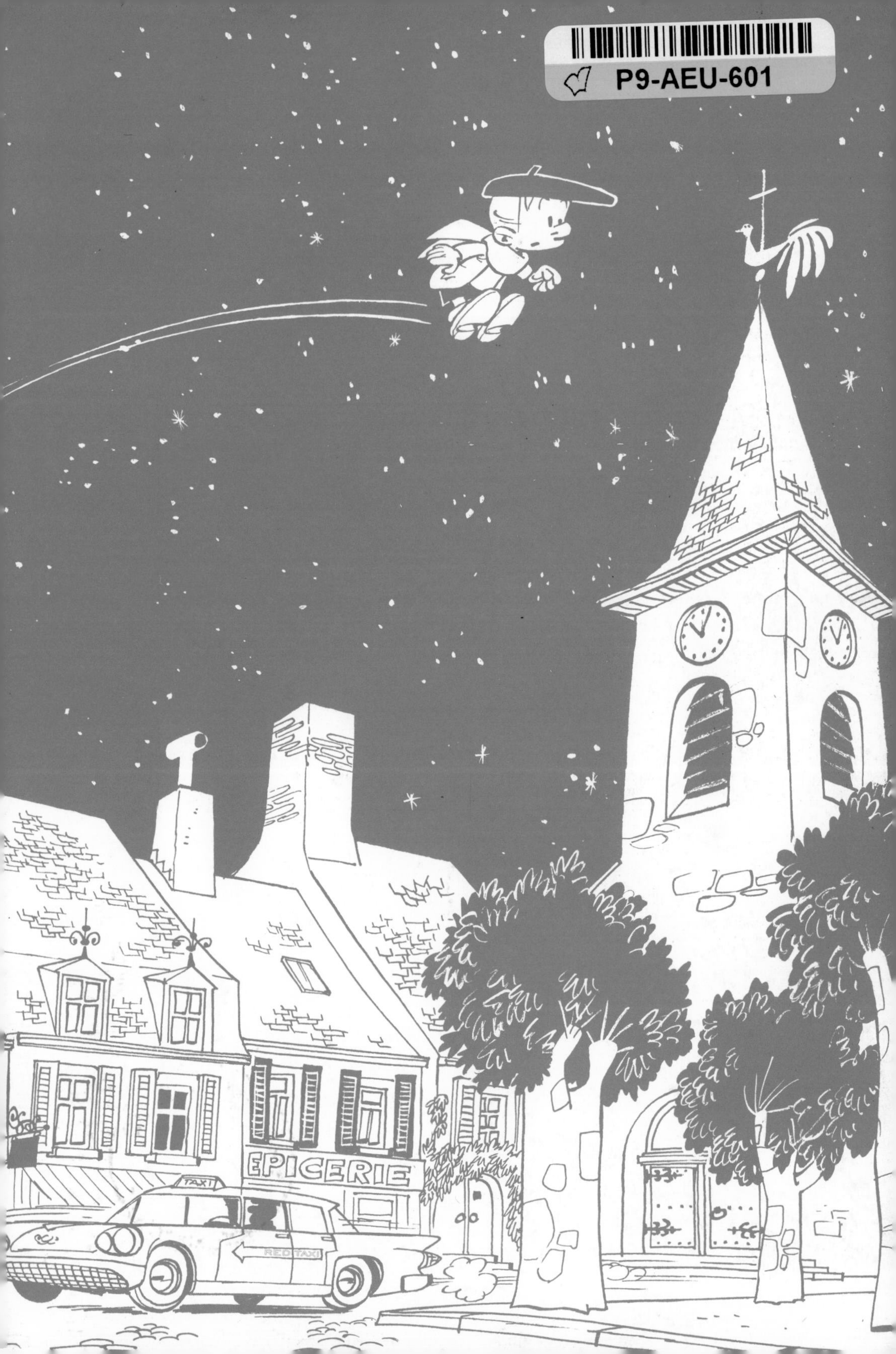
EPICERIE
TAXI
RED TAXI

BENNY BREAKIRON

IN

THE RED TAXIS

BY

Peyo

WITH BACKGROUNDS BY Will

PAPERCUTZ™

NEW YORK

Peyo GRAPHIC NOVELS AVAILABLE FROM PAPERCUTZ™

BENNY BREAKIRON

THE SMURFS

BENNY BREAKIRON graphic novels are available in hardcover only for $11.99 each. THE SMURFS graphic novels are available in paperback for $5.99 each and in hardcover for $10.99 each at booksellers everywhere. You can also order online at www.papercutz.com. Or call 1-800-886-1223, Monday through Fridays, 9 – 5 EST. MC, Visa, and AmEx accepted. To order by mail, please add $4.00 for postage and handling for first book ordered, $1.00 for each additional book and make check payable to NBM Publishing. Send to: Papercutz, 160 Broadway, Suite 700, East Wing, New York, NY 10038.

BENNY BREAKIRON and THE SMURFS graphic novels are also available digitally wherever e-books are sold.

WWW.PAPERCUTZ.COM

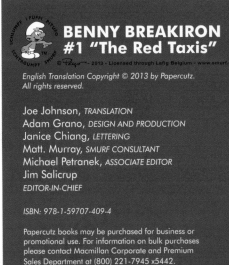

BENNY BREAKIRON
#1 "The Red Taxis"

© Peyo - 2013 - Licensed through Lafig Belgium - www.smurf.com

*English Translation Copyright © 2013 by Papercutz.
All rights reserved.*

Joe Johnson, TRANSLATION
Adam Grano, DESIGN AND PRODUCTION
Janice Chiang, LETTERING
Matt. Murray, SMURF CONSULTANT
Michael Petranek, ASSOCIATE EDITOR
Jim Salicrup
EDITOR-IN-CHIEF

ISBN: 978-1-59707-409-4

Papercutz books may be purchased for business or promotional use. For information on bulk purchases please contact Macmillan Corporate and Premium Sales Department at (800) 221-7945 x5442.

*PRINTED IN CHINA MAY 2013 BY NEW ERA PRINTING, LTD
UNIT C, 8/F, WORLDWIDE CENTRE, 123 TUNG CHAU ST.
KOWLOON, HONG KONG*

*DISTRIBUTED BY MACMILLAN
FIRST PAPERCUTZ PRINTING*

THE RED TAXIS

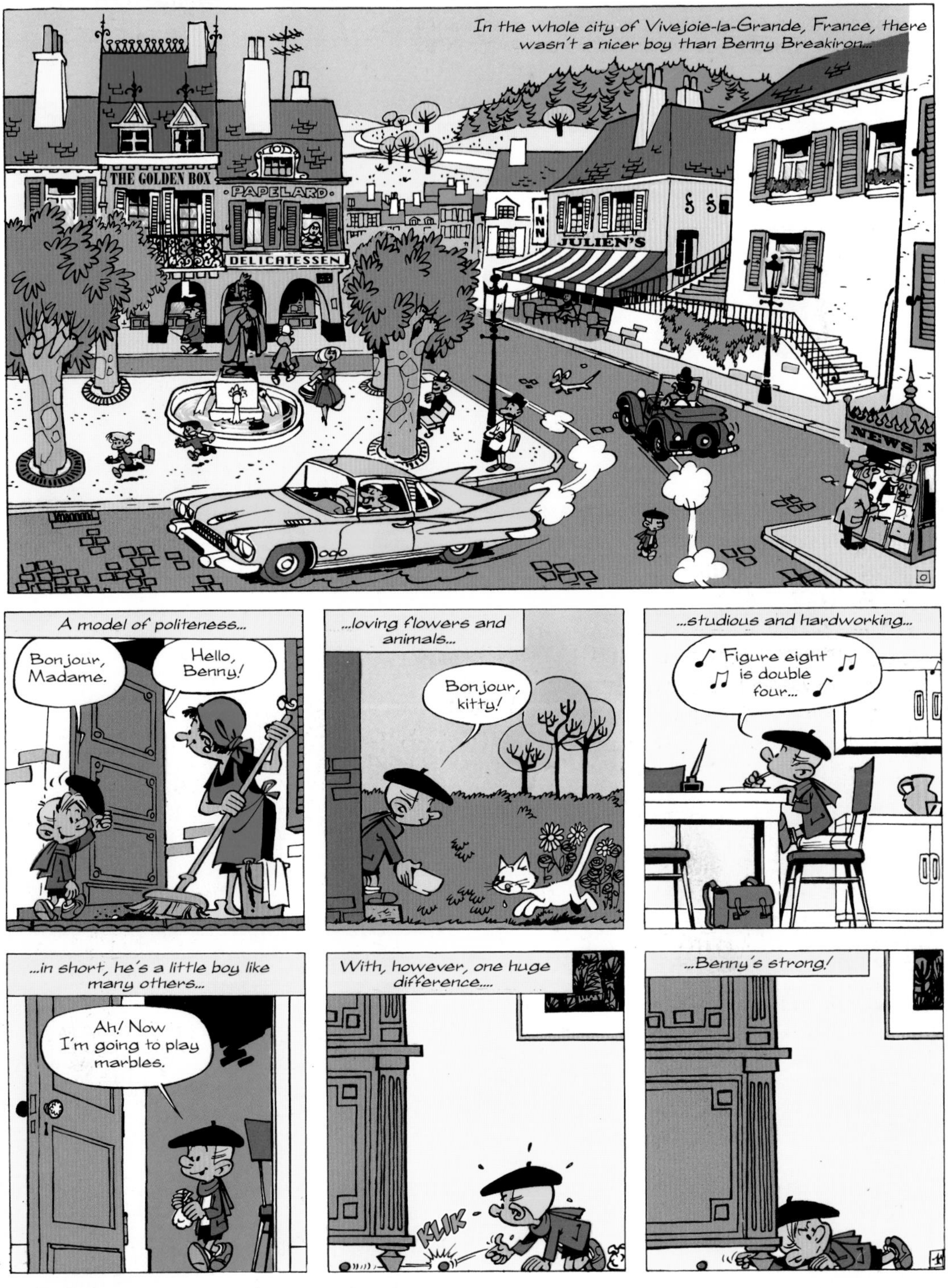

In the whole city of Vivejoie-la-Grande, France, there wasn't a nicer boy than Benny Breakiron...
THE GOLDEN BOX
PAPELARD
DELICATESSEN
INN
JULIEN'S
NEWS
A model of politeness...
Bonjour, Madame.
Hello, Benny!
...loving flowers and animals...
Bonjour, kitty!
...studious and hardworking...
Figure eight is double four...
...in short, he's a little boy like many others...
Ah! Now I'm going to play marbles.
With, however, one huge difference....
KLIK
...Benny's strong!

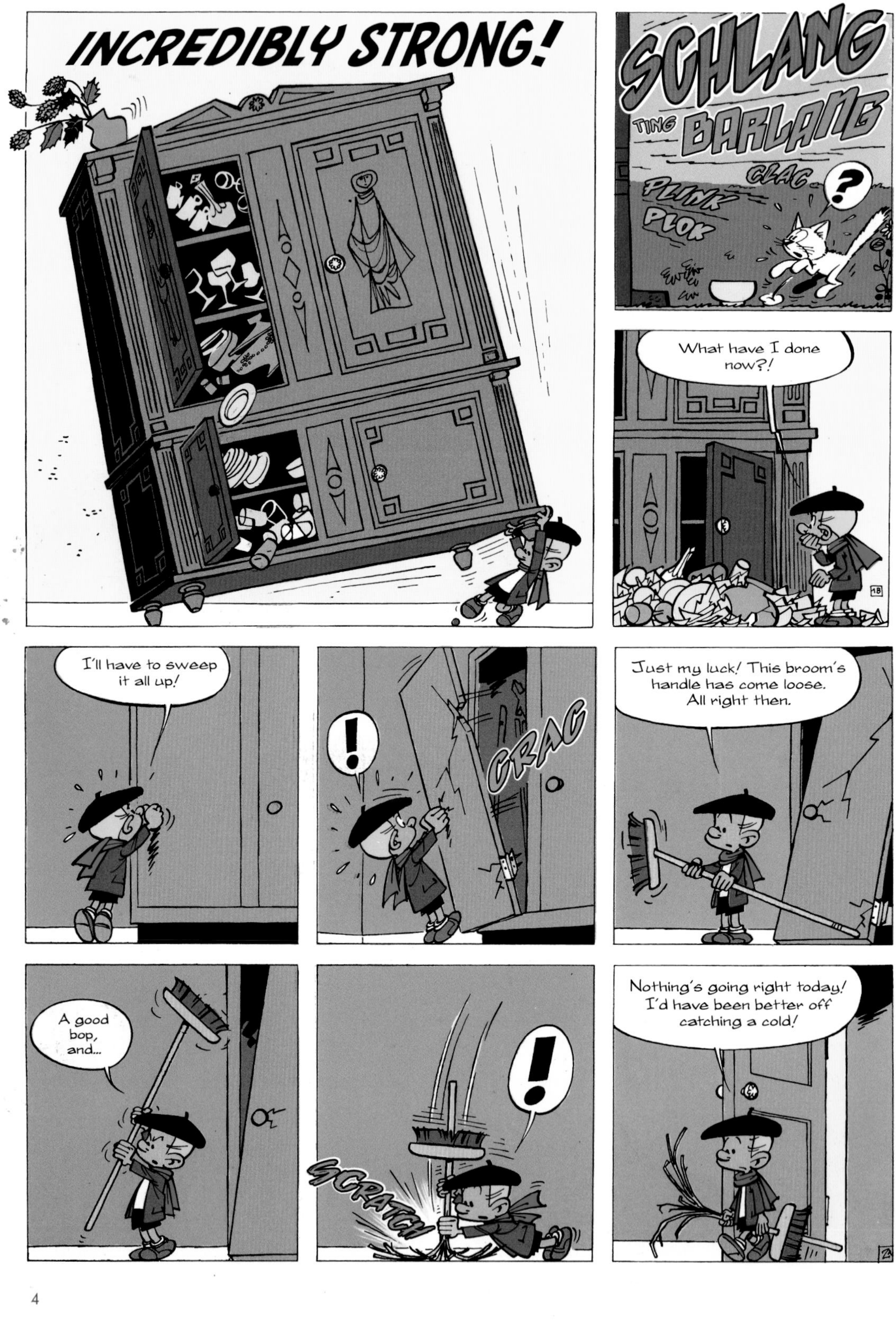
INCREDIBLY STRONG!
SCHLANG
TING
BARLANG
CLAC
PLINK
PLOK
?
What have I done now?!
I'll have to sweep it all up!
!
CRAC
Just my luck! This broom's handle has come loose. All right then.
A good bop, and...
SCRATCH
!
Nothing's going right today! I'd have been better off catching a cold!

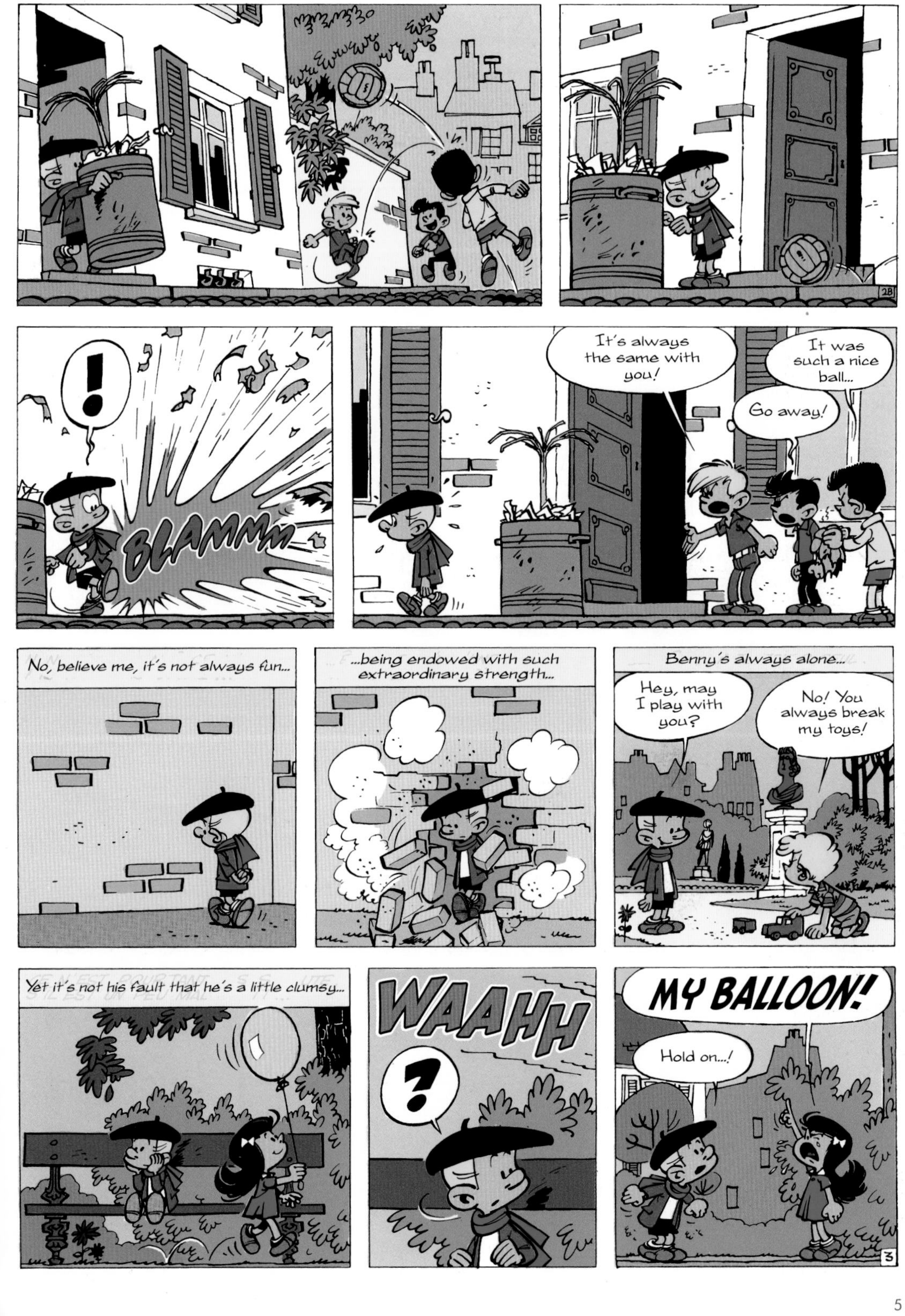
2B
BLAMMM
It's always the same with you!
It was such a nice ball...
Go away!
No, believe me, it's not always fun...
...being endowed with such extraordinary strength...
Benny's always alone...
Hey, may I play with you?
No! You always break my toys!
Yet it's not his fault that he's a little clumsy...
WAAHH
MY BALLOON!
Hold on...!
3

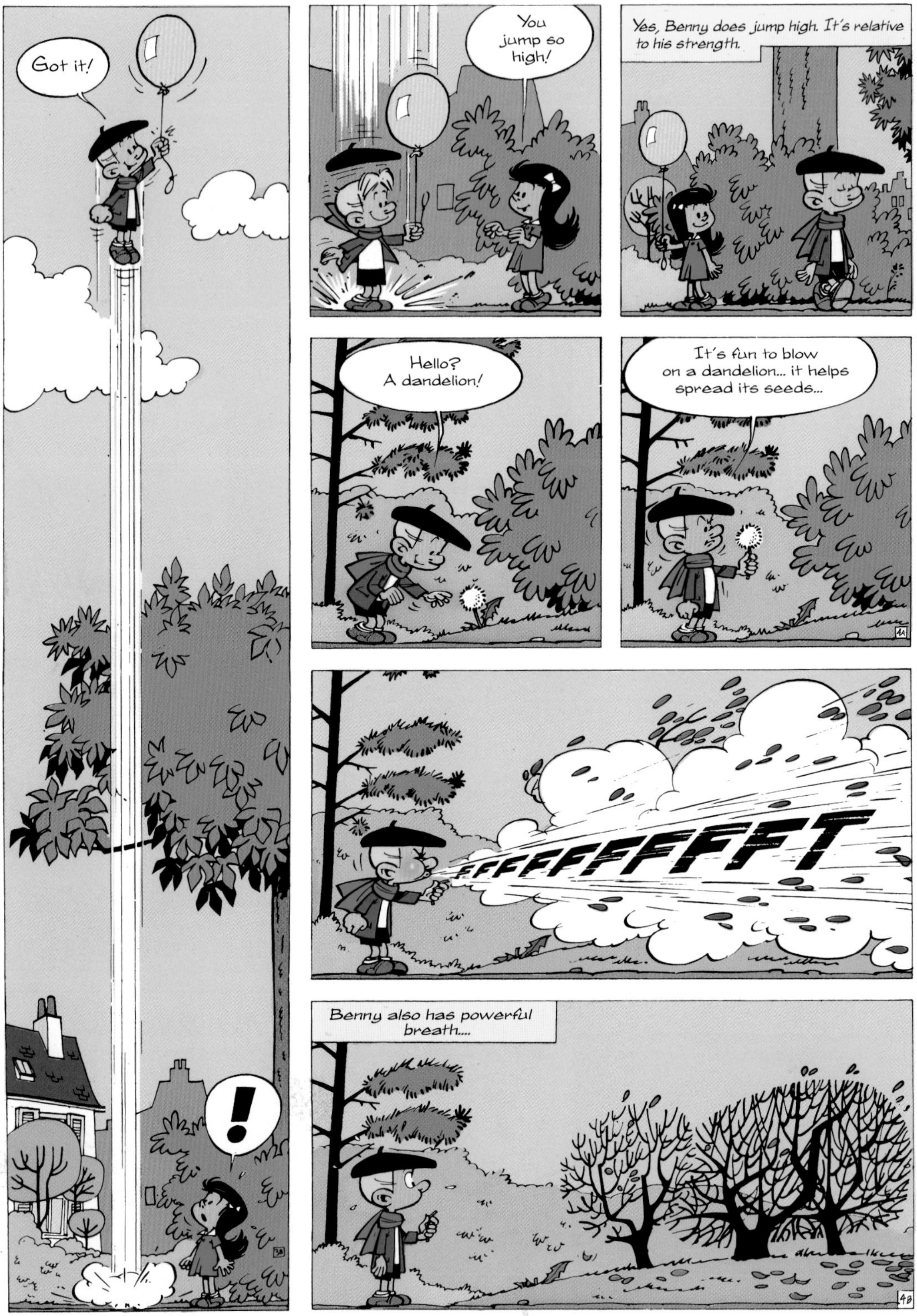
Got it!
!
You jump so high!
Yes, Benny does jump high. It's relative to his strength.
Hello? A dandelion!
It's fun to blow on a dandelion... it helps spread its seeds...
FFFFFFFFFFFT
Benny also has powerful breath....

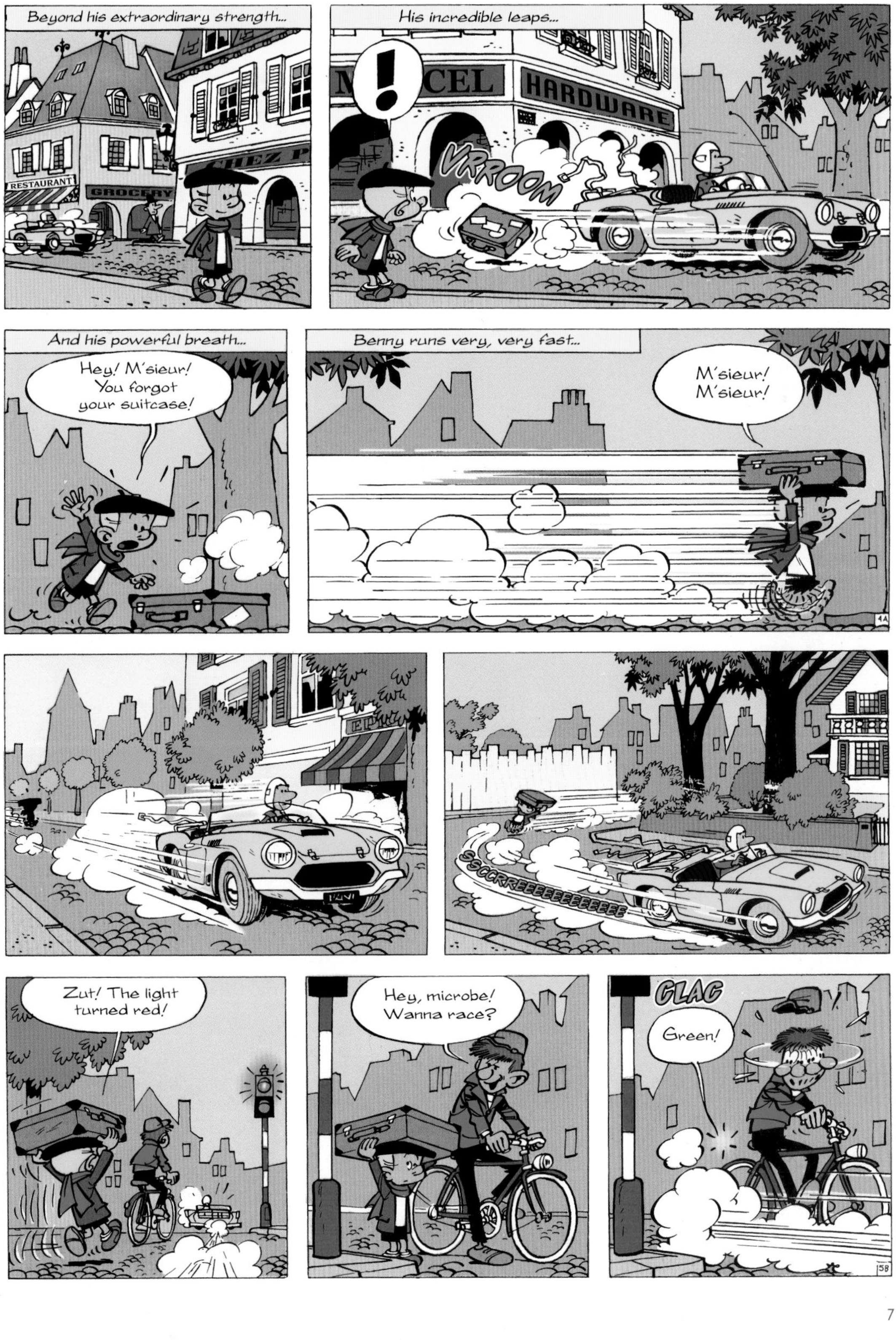
Beyond his extraordinary strength...
RESTAURANT
GROCERY
His incredible leaps...
!
HARDWARE
VRROOM
And his powerful breath...
Hey! M'sieur! You forgot your suitcase!
Benny runs very, very fast...
M'sieur! M'sieur!
SSCCRREEEEEEEEEEEEE
Zut! The light turned red!
Hey, microbe! Wanna race?
CLAG
Green!

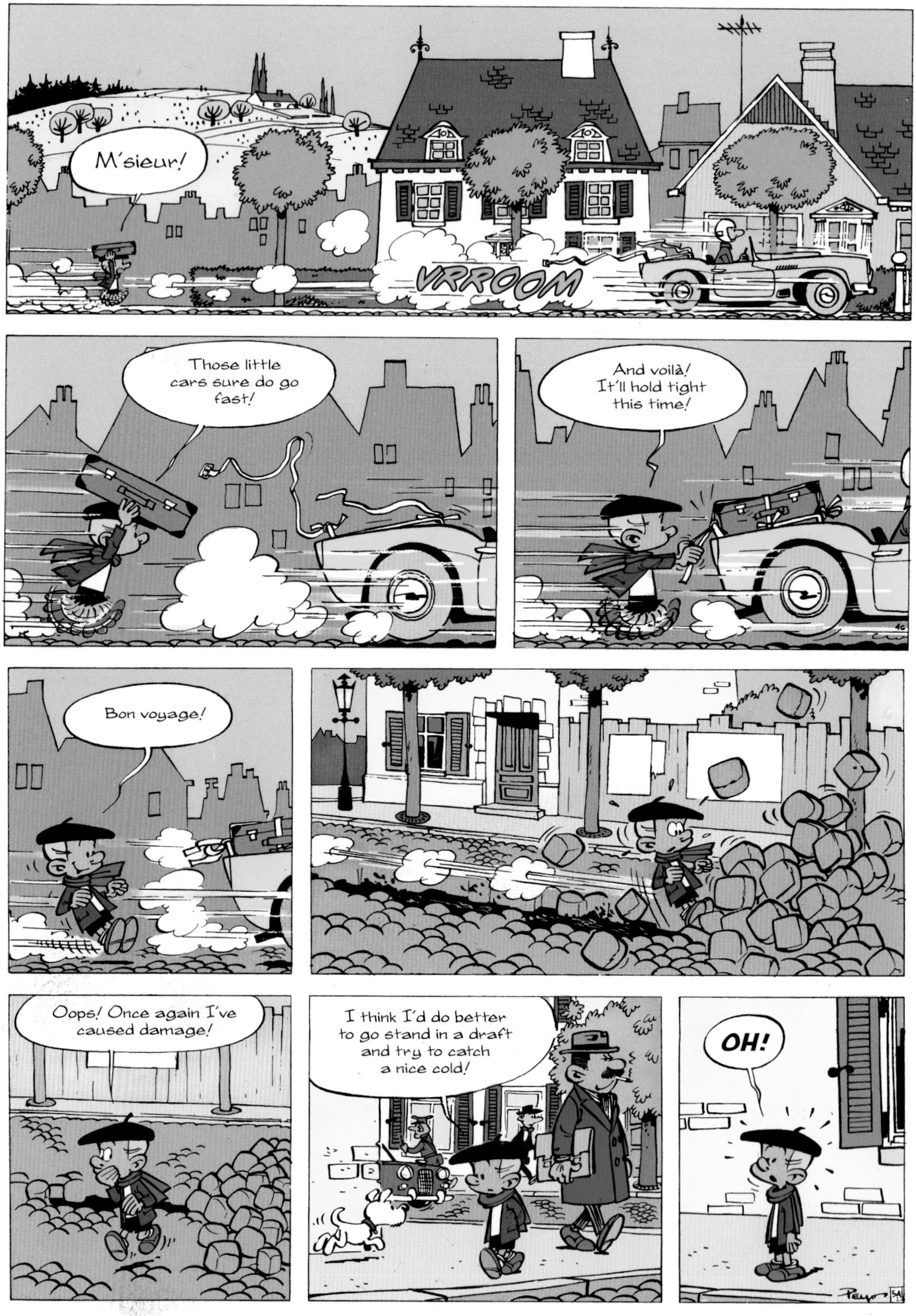
M'sieur!
VRROOM
Those little cars sure do go fast!
And voilà! It'll hold tight this time!
Bon voyage!
Oops! Once again I've caused damage!
I think I'd do better to go stand in a draft and try to catch a nice cold!
OH!
Peyo

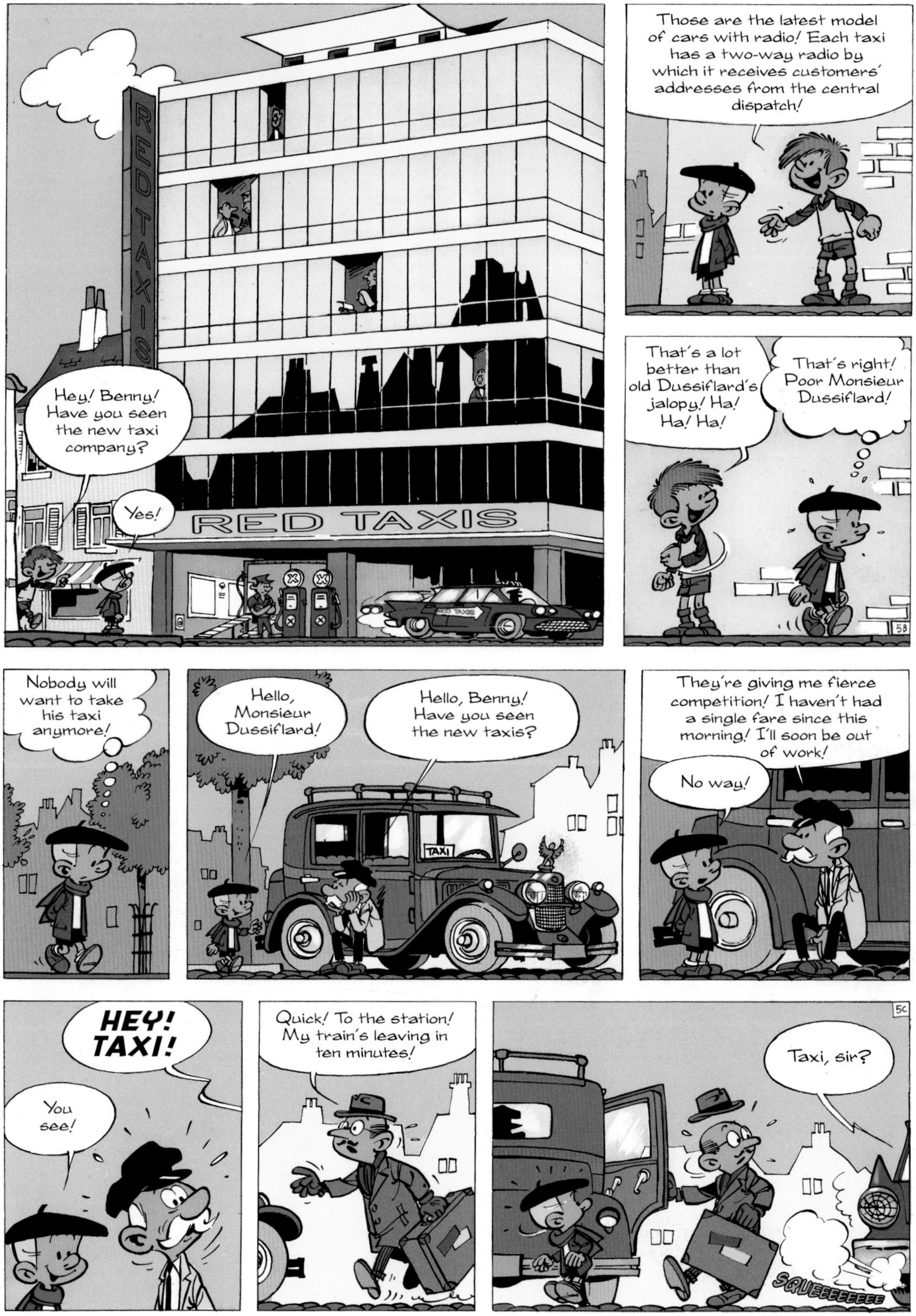
RED TAXIS
Hey! Benny! Have you seen the new taxi company?
Yes!
RED TAXIS
Those are the latest model of cars with radio! Each taxi has a two-way radio by which it receives customers' addresses from the central dispatch!
That's a lot better than old Dussiflard's jalopy! Ha! Ha! Ha!
That's right! Poor Monsieur Dussiflard!
5B
Nobody will want to take his taxi anymore!
Hello, Monsieur Dussiflard!
Hello, Benny! Have you seen the new taxis?
TAXI
They're giving me fierce competition! I haven't had a single fare since this morning! I'll soon be out of work!
No way!
HEY! TAXI!
You see!
Quick! To the station! My train's leaving in ten minutes!
5C
Taxi, sir?
SQUEEEEEEEE

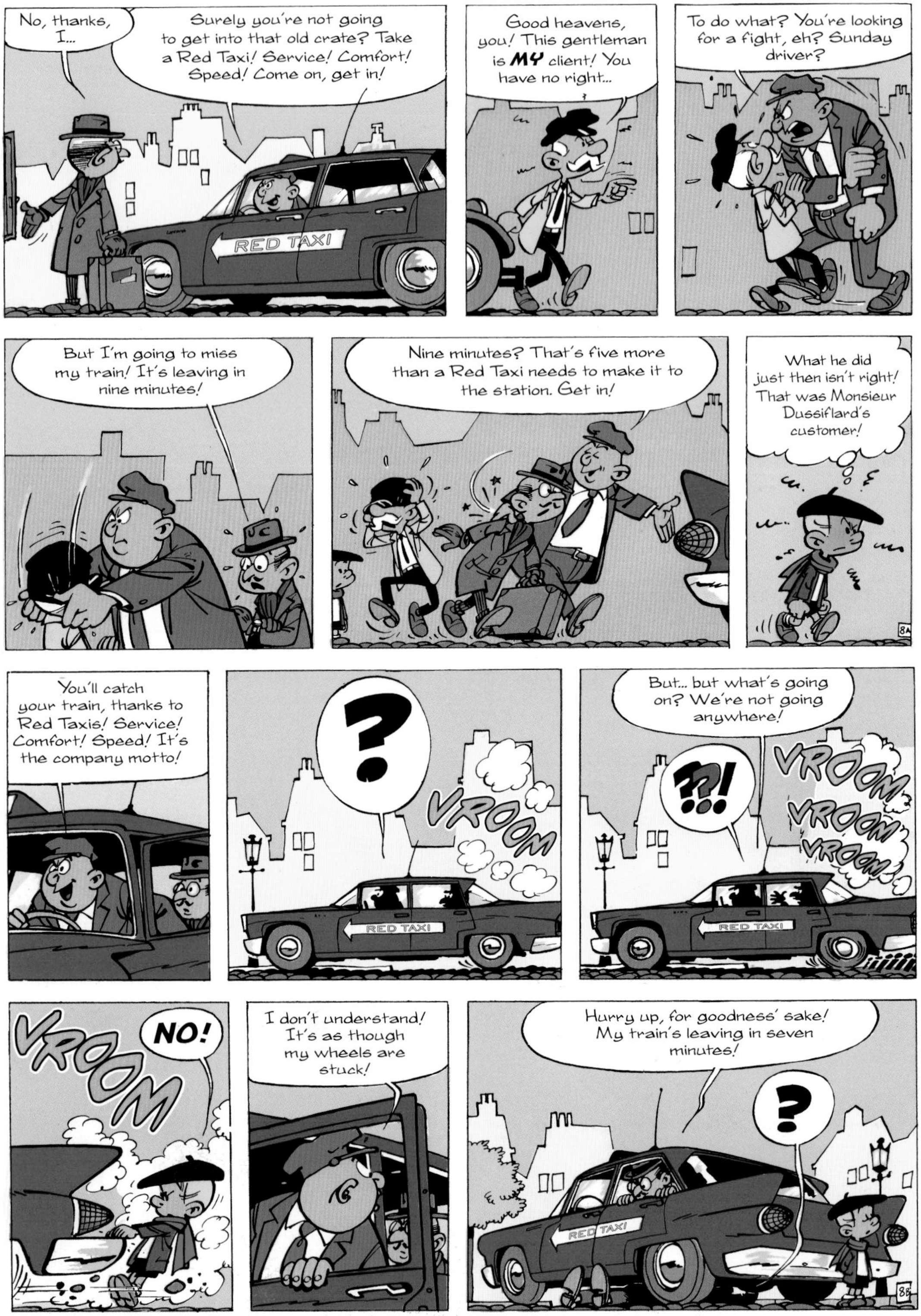
No, thanks, I...
Surely you're not going to get into that old crate? Take a Red Taxi! Service! Comfort! Speed! Come on, get in!
RED TAXI
Good heavens, you! This gentleman is MY client! You have no right...
To do what? You're looking for a fight, eh? Sunday driver?
But I'm going to miss my train! It's leaving in nine minutes!
Nine minutes? That's five more than a Red Taxi needs to make it to the station. Get in!
What he did just then isn't right! That was Monsieur Dussiflard's customer!
You'll catch your train, thanks to Red Taxis! Service! Comfort! Speed! It's the company motto!
?
VROOM
RED TAXI
But... but what's going on? We're not going anywhere!
??!
VROOM
VROOM
VROOM
RED TAXI
VROOM
NO!
I don't understand! It's as though my wheels are stuck!
Hurry up, for goodness' sake! My train's leaving in seven minutes!
?
RED TAXI

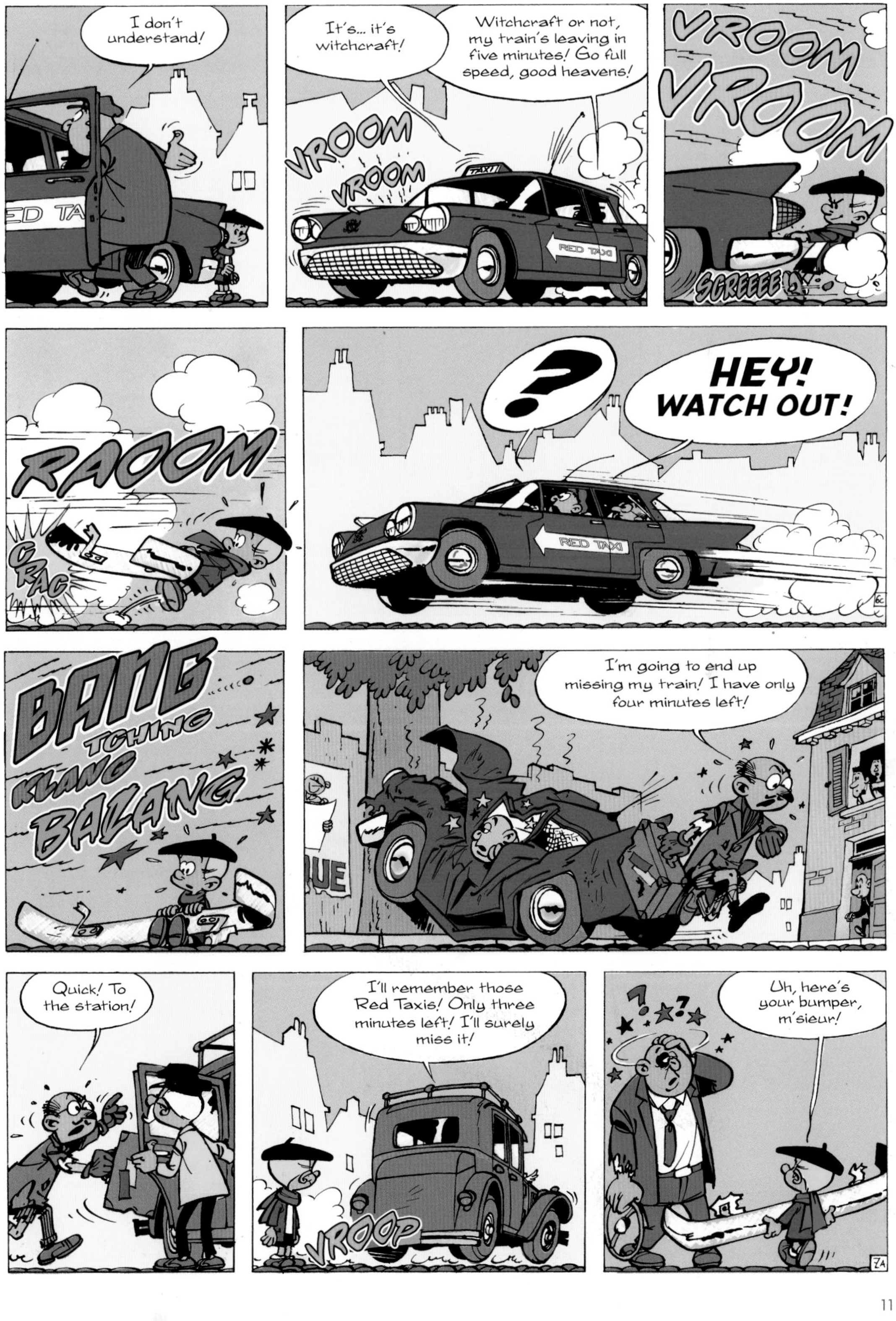
I don't understand!
RED TA
It's... it's witchcraft!
Witchcraft or not, my train's leaving in five minutes! Go full speed, good heavens!
VROOM
VROOM
TAXI
RED TAXI
VROOM
VROOM
SCREEEE
RAOOM
CRAC
?
HEY! WATCH OUT!
RED TAXI
BANG
TCHING
KLANG
BALANG
I'm going to end up missing my train! I have only four minutes left!
QUE
Quick! To the station!
I'll remember those Red Taxis! Only three minutes left! I'll surely miss it!
VROOP
Uh, here's your bumper, m'sieur!

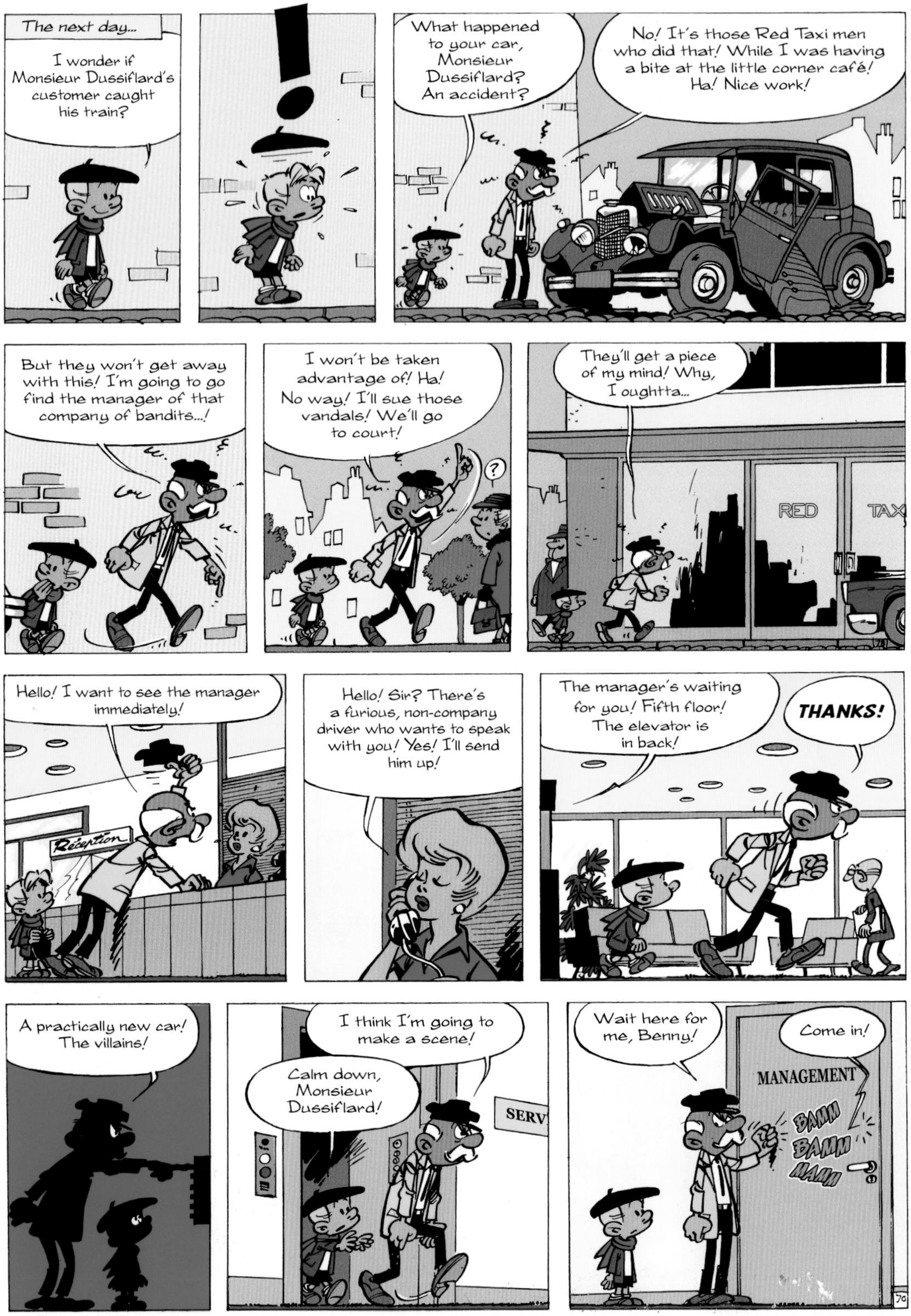

The next day...
I wonder if Monsieur Dussiflard's customer caught his train?
!
What happened to your car, Monsieur Dussiflard? An accident?
No! It's those Red Taxi men who did that! While I was having a bite at the little corner café! Ha! Nice work!
But they won't get away with this! I'm going to go find the manager of that company of bandits...!
I won't be taken advantage of! Ha! No way! I'll sue those vandals! We'll go to court!
?
They'll get a piece of my mind! Why, I oughtta...
RED
TAX
Hello! I want to see the manager immediately!
Reception
Hello! Sir? There's a furious, non-company driver who wants to speak with you! Yes! I'll send him up!
The manager's waiting for you! Fifth floor! The elevator is in back!
THANKS!
A practically new car! The villains!
I think I'm going to make a scene!
Calm down, Monsieur Dussiflard!
SERV
Wait here for me, Benny!
Come in!
MANAGEMENT
BAMM
BAMM
MAMM

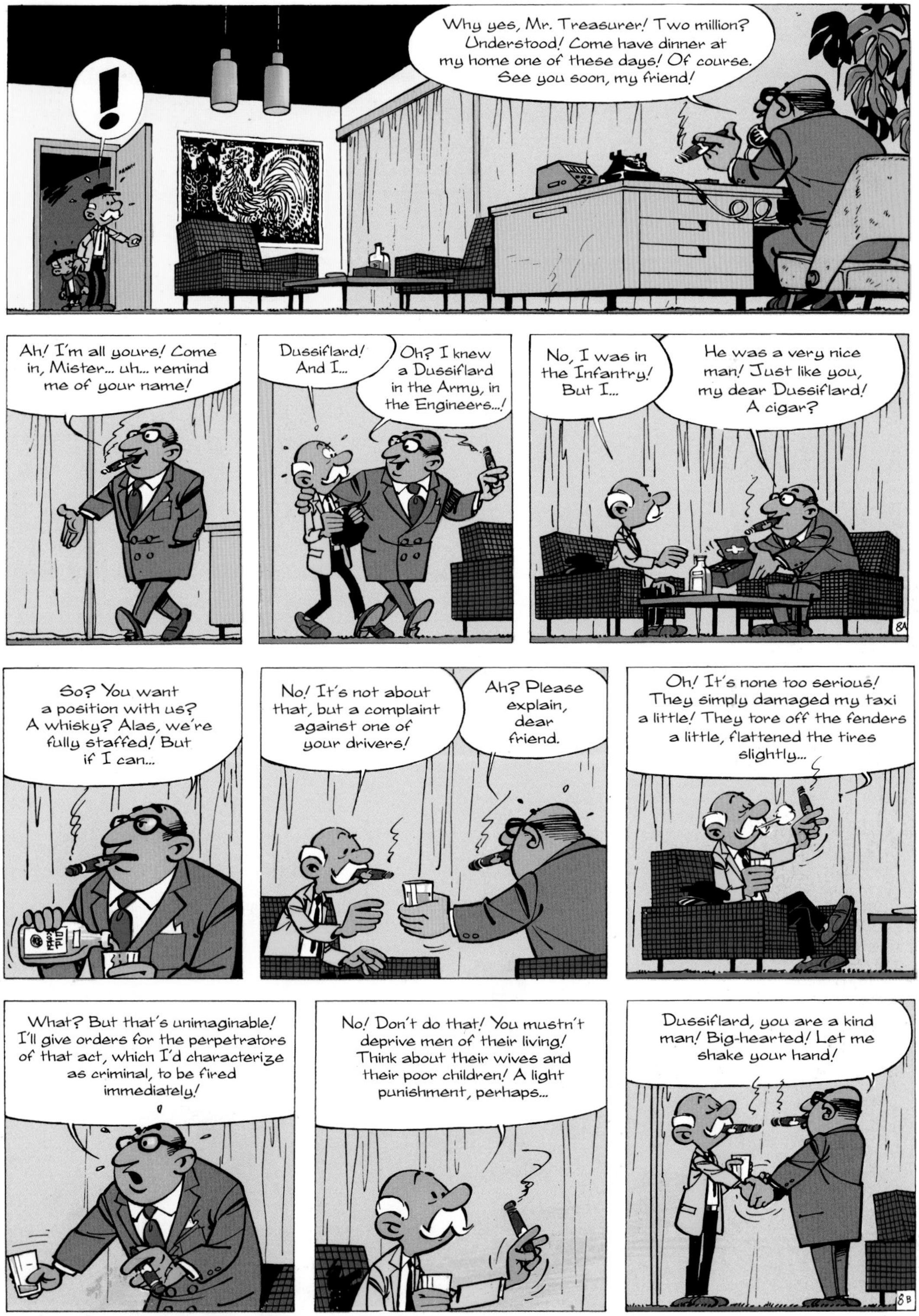
Why yes, Mr. Treasurer! Two million? Understood! Come have dinner at my home one of these days! Of course. See you soon, my friend!
!
Ah! I'm all yours! Come in, Mister... uh... remind me of your name!
Dussiflard! And I...
Oh? I knew a Dussiflard in the Army, in the Engineers...!
No, I was in the Infantry! But I...
He was a very nice man! Just like you, my dear Dussiflard! A cigar?
So? You want a position with us? A whisky? Alas, we're fully staffed! But if I can...
No! It's not about that, but a complaint against one of your drivers!
Ah? Please explain, dear friend.
Oh! It's none too serious! They simply damaged my taxi a little! They tore off the fenders a little, flattened the tires slightly...
What? But that's unimaginable! I'll give orders for the perpetrators of that act, which I'd characterize as criminal, to be fired immediately!
No! Don't do that! You mustn't deprive men of their living! Think about their wives and their poor children! A light punishment, perhaps...
Dussiflard, you are a kind man! Big-hearted! Let me shake your hand!

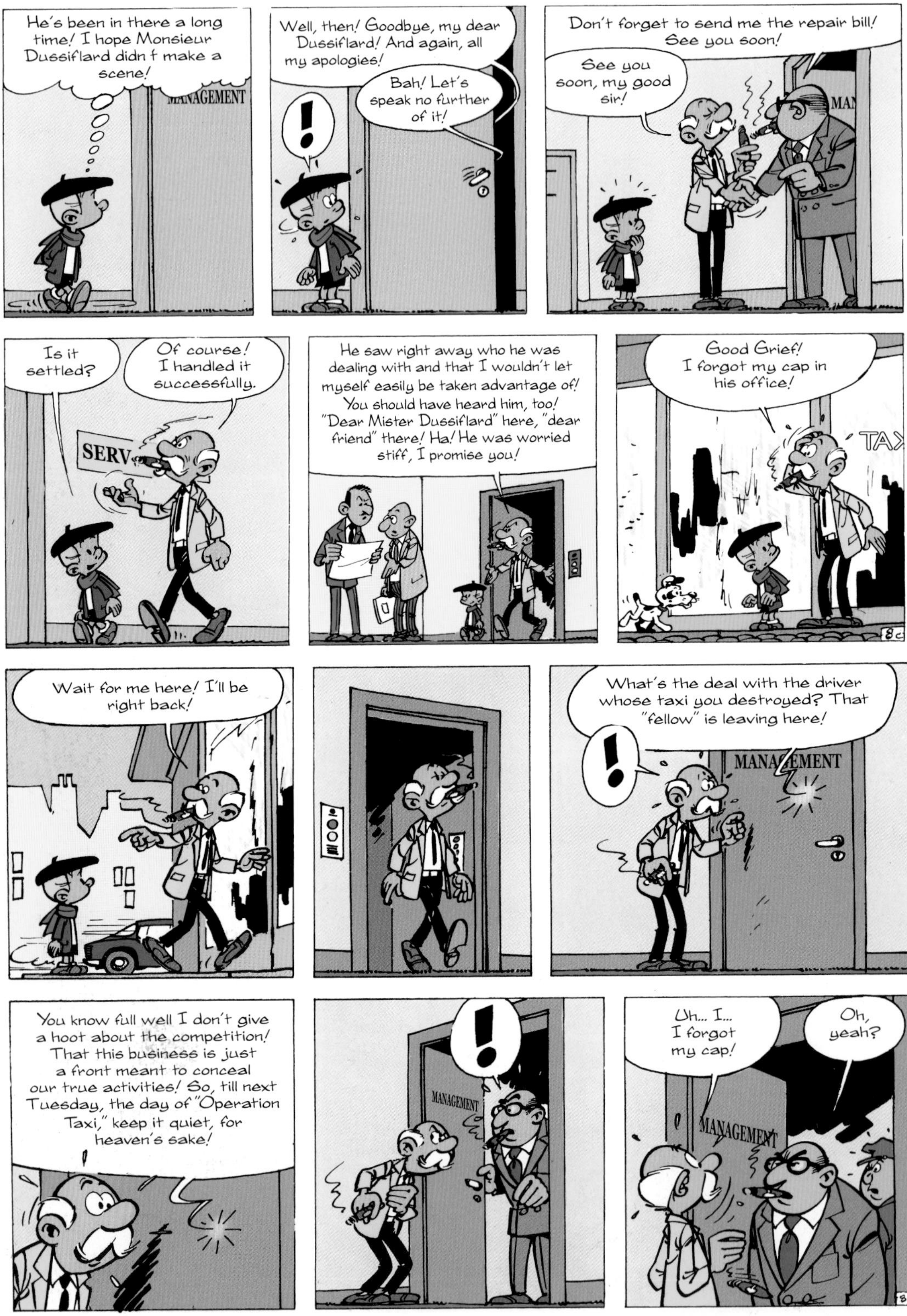

He's been in there a long time! I hope Monsieur Dussiflard didn't make a scene!
MANAGEMENT
Well, then! Goodbye, my dear Dussiflard! And again, all my apologies!
!
Bah! Let's speak no further of it!
Don't forget to send me the repair bill! See you soon!
See you soon, my good sir!
MAN
Is it settled?
Of course! I handled it successfully.
SERV
He saw right away who he was dealing with and that I wouldn't let myself easily be taken advantage of! You should have heard him, too! "Dear Mister Dussiflard" here, "dear friend" there! Ha! He was worried stiff, I promise you!
Good Grief! I forgot my cap in his office!
TAX
Wait for me here! I'll be right back!
What's the deal with the driver whose taxi you destroyed? That "fellow" is leaving here!
!
MANAGEMENT
You know full well I don't give a hoot about the competition! That this business is just a front meant to conceal our true activities! So, till next Tuesday, the day of "Operation Taxi," keep it quiet, for heaven's sake!
!
MANAGEMENT
Uh... I... I forgot my cap!
Oh, yeah?
MANAGEMENT

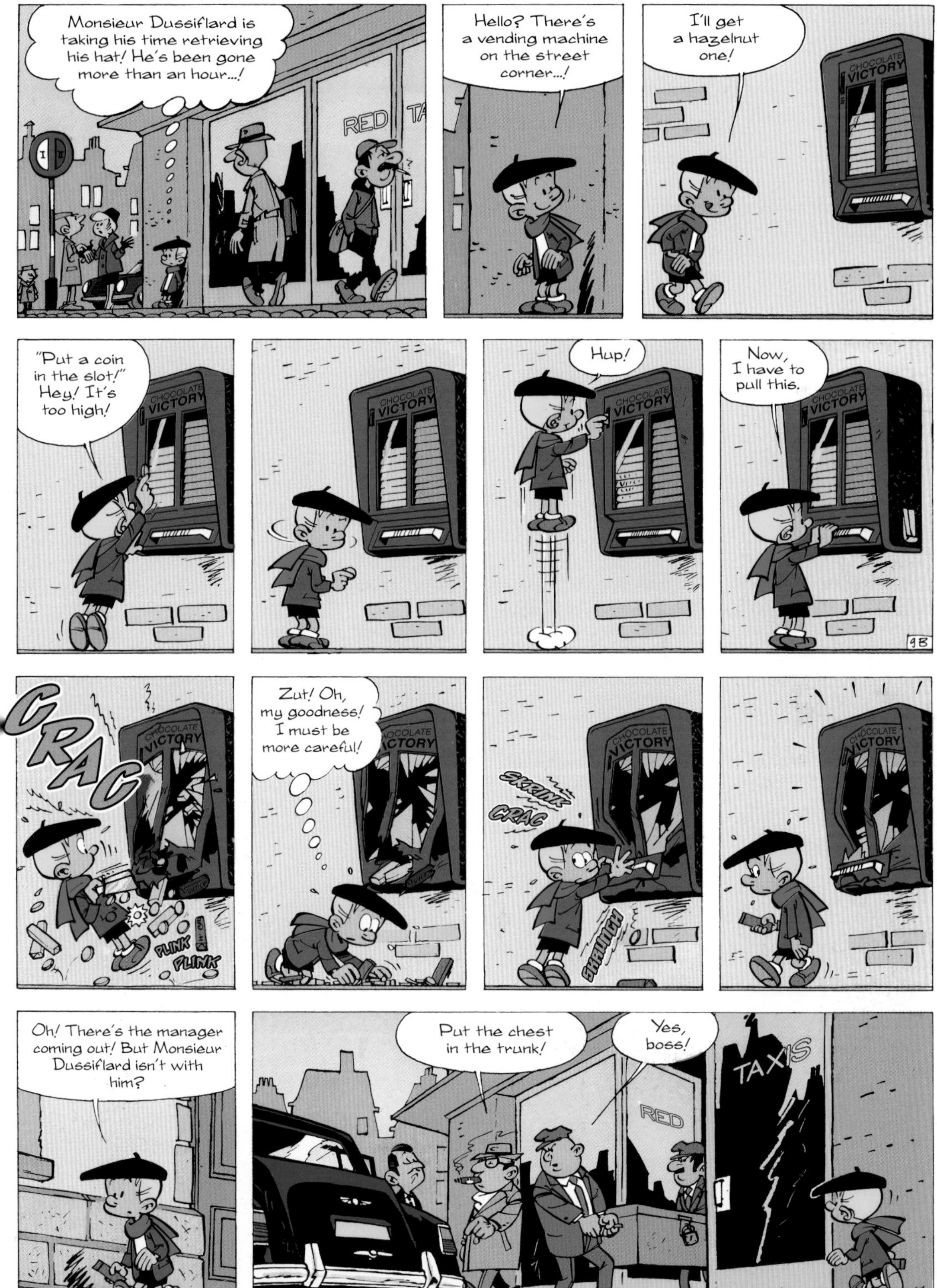
Monsieur Dussiflard is taking his time retrieving his hat! He's been gone more than an hour...!
RED
Hello? There's a vending machine on the street corner...!
I'll get a hazelnut one!
CHOCOLATE VICTORY
"Put a coin in the slot!" Hey! It's too high!
Hup!
Now, I have to pull this.
9B
CRAC
PLINK
PLINK
Zut! Oh, my goodness! I must be more careful!
SKRINK
CRAC
SHRUNCH
Oh! There's the manager coming out! But Monsieur Dussiflard isn't with him?
Put the chest in the trunk!
Yes, boss!
RED
TAXIS
9C

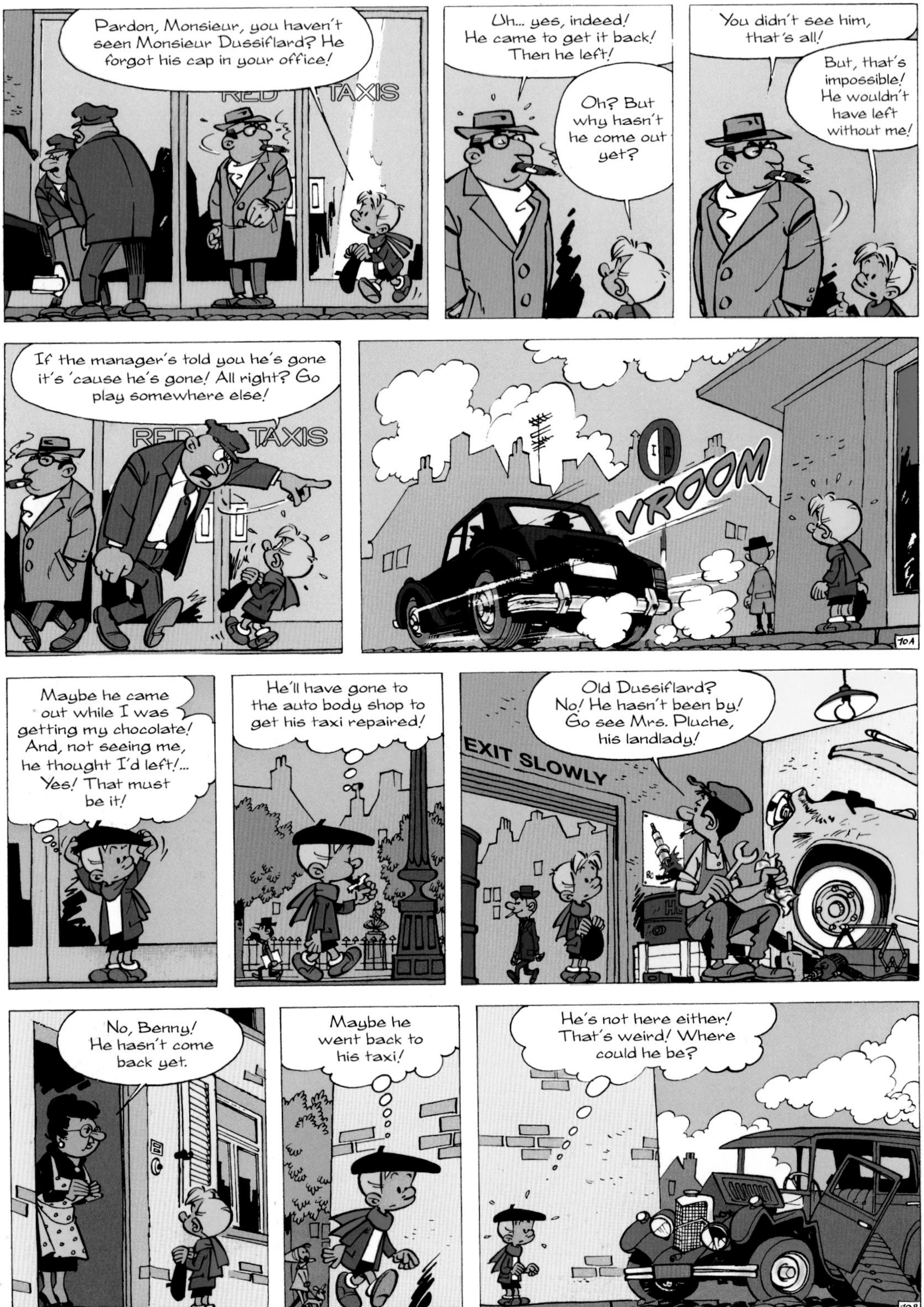

Pardon, Monsieur, you haven't seen Monsieur Dussiflard? He forgot his cap in your office!
RED TAXIS
Uh... yes, indeed! He came to get it back! Then he left!
Oh? But why hasn't he come out yet?
You didn't see him, that's all!
But, that's impossible! He wouldn't have left without me!
If the manager's told you he's gone it's 'cause he's gone! All right? Go play somewhere else!
RED TAXIS
VROOM
10A
Maybe he came out while I was getting my chocolate! And, not seeing me, he thought I'd left!... Yes! That must be it!
He'll have gone to the auto body shop to get his taxi repaired!
Old Dussiflard? No! He hasn't been by! Go see Mrs. Pluche, his landlady!
EXIT SLOWLY
No, Benny! He hasn't come back yet.
Maybe he went back to his taxi!
He's not here either! That's weird! Where could he be?
10B

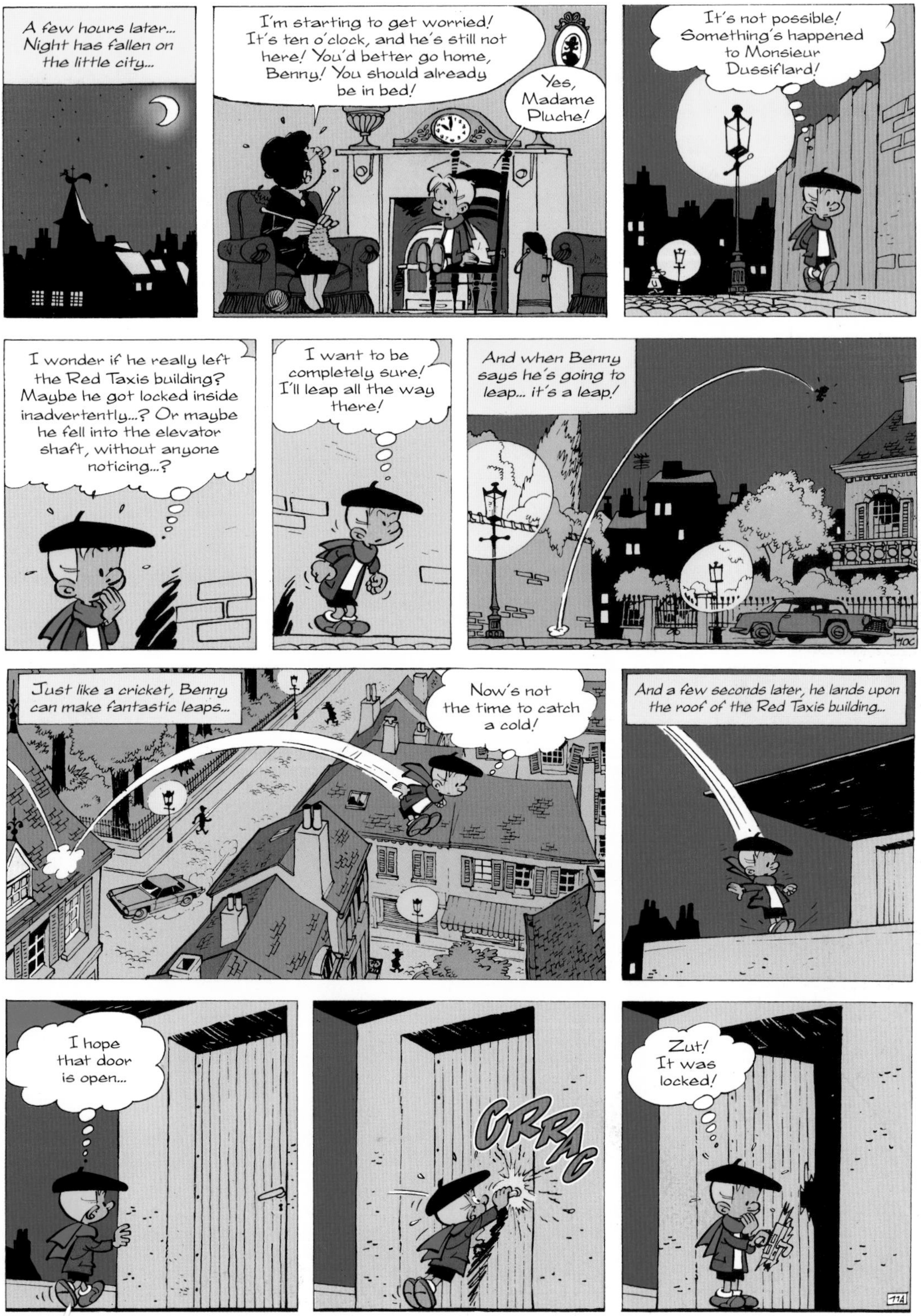
A few hours later... Night has fallen on the little city...
I'm starting to get worried! It's ten o'clock, and he's still not here! You'd better go home, Benny! You should already be in bed!
Yes, Madame Pluche!
It's not possible! Something's happened to Monsieur Dussiflard!
I wonder if he really left the Red Taxis building? Maybe he got locked inside inadvertently...? Or maybe he fell into the elevator shaft, without anyone noticing...?
I want to be completely sure! I'll leap all the way there!
And when Benny says he's going to leap... it's a leap!
Just like a cricket, Benny can make fantastic leaps...
Now's not the time to catch a cold!
And a few seconds later, he lands upon the roof of the Red Taxis building...
I hope that door is open...
CRRAC
Zut! It was locked!

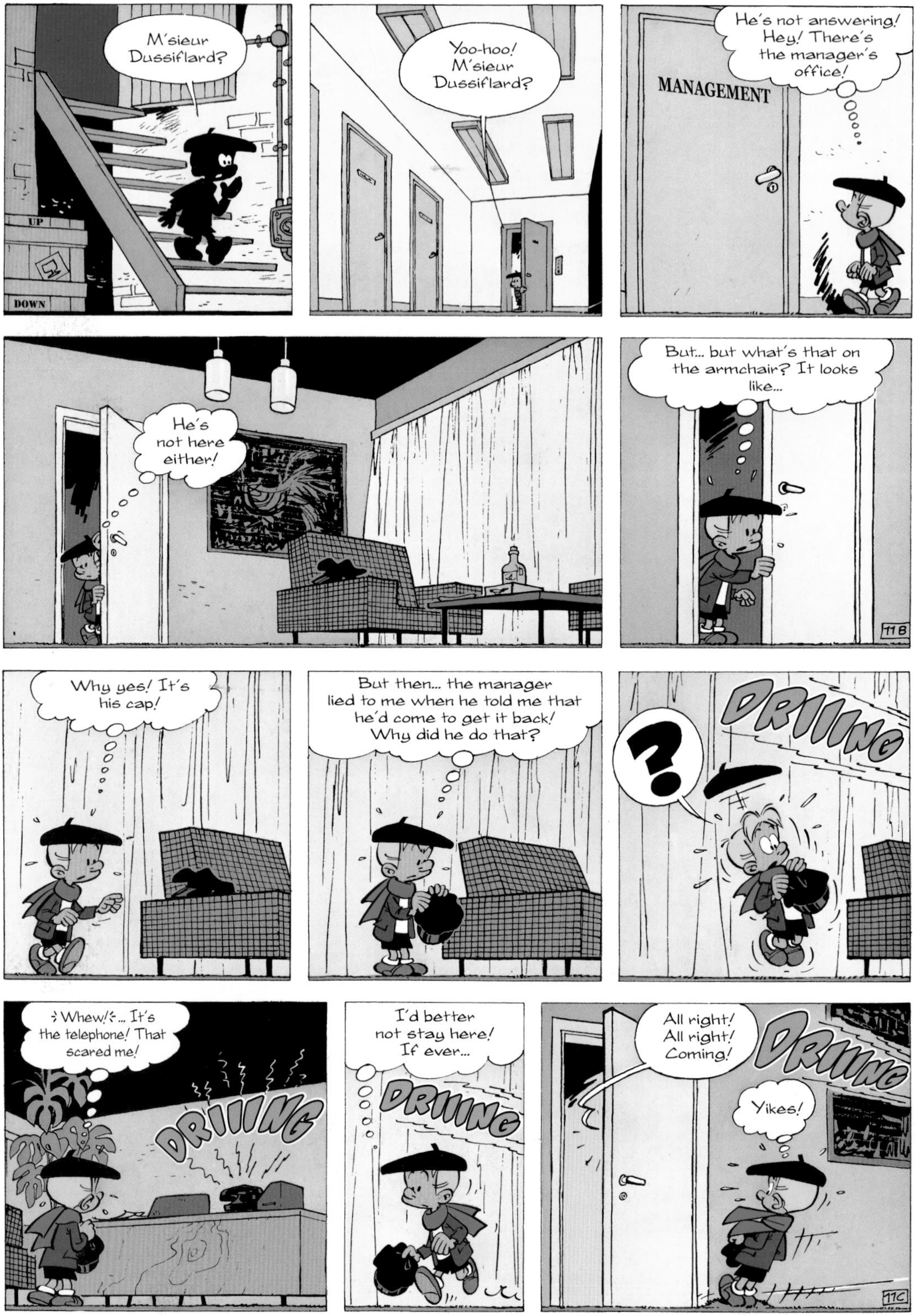
M'sieur Dussiflard?
UP
DOWN
Yoo-hoo! M'sieur Dussiflard?
He's not answering! Hey! There's the manager's office!
MANAGEMENT
He's not here either!
But... but what's that on the armchair? It looks like...
11 B
Why yes! It's his cap!
But then... the manager lied to me when he told me that he'd come to get it back! Why did he do that?
DRIIING
?
Whew!... It's the telephone! That scared me!
DRIIIING
I'd better not stay here! If ever...
DRIIING
All right! All right! Coming!
DRIIING
Yikes!
11C

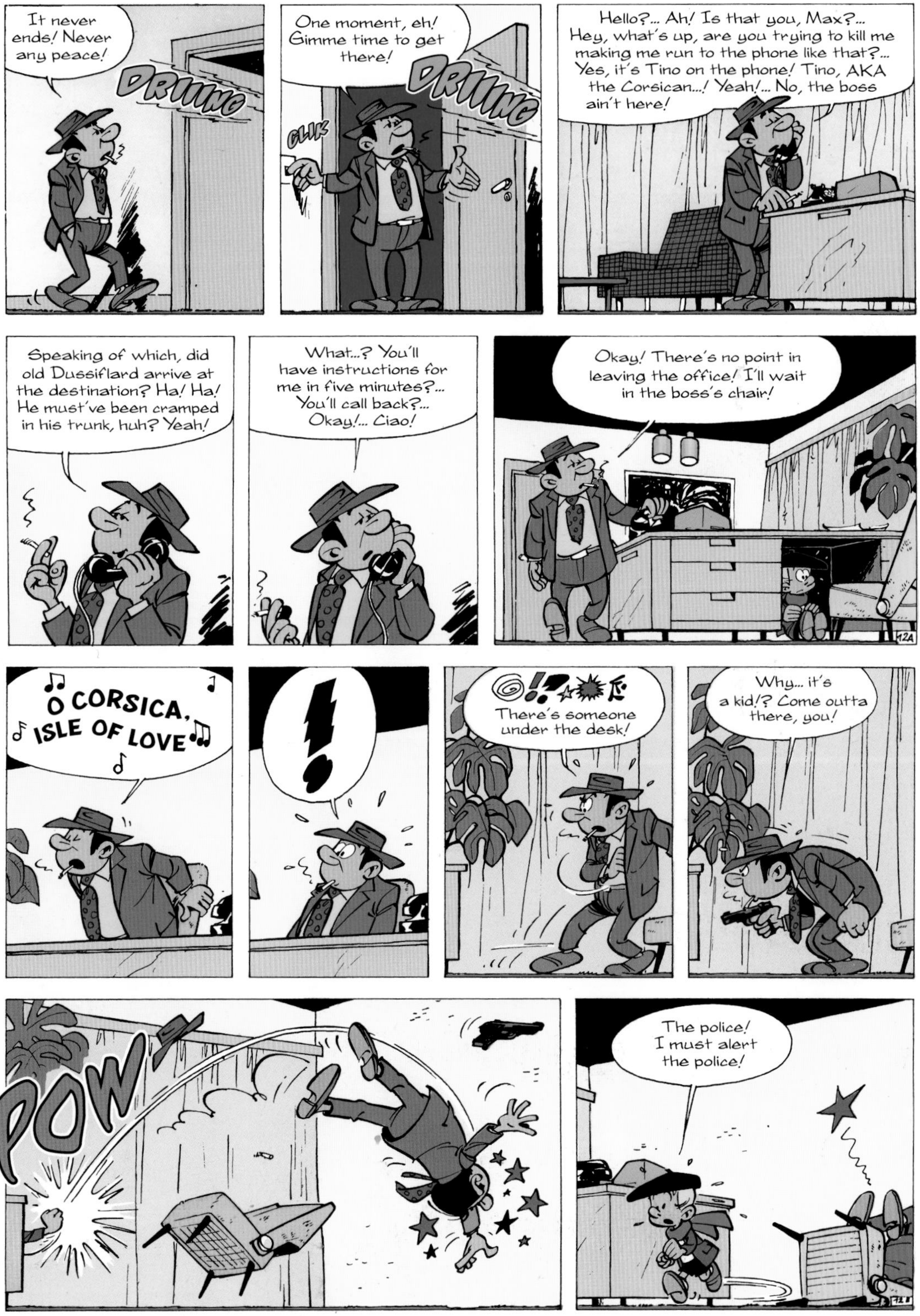
It never ends! Never any peace!
DRIIING
One moment, eh! Gimme time to get there!
DRIIING
CLIK
Hello?... Ah! Is that you, Max?... Hey, what's up, are you trying to kill me making me run to the phone like that?... Yes, it's Tino on the phone! Tino, AKA the Corsican...! Yeah!... No, the boss ain't here!
Speaking of which, did old Dussiflard arrive at the destination? Ha! Ha! He must've been cramped in his trunk, huh? Yeah!
What...? You'll have instructions for me in five minutes?... You'll call back?... Okay!... Ciao!
Okay! There's no point in leaving the office! I'll wait in the boss's chair!
O CORSICA, ISLE OF LOVE
!
There's someone under the desk!
Why... it's a kid!? Come outta there, you!
POW
The police! I must alert the police!

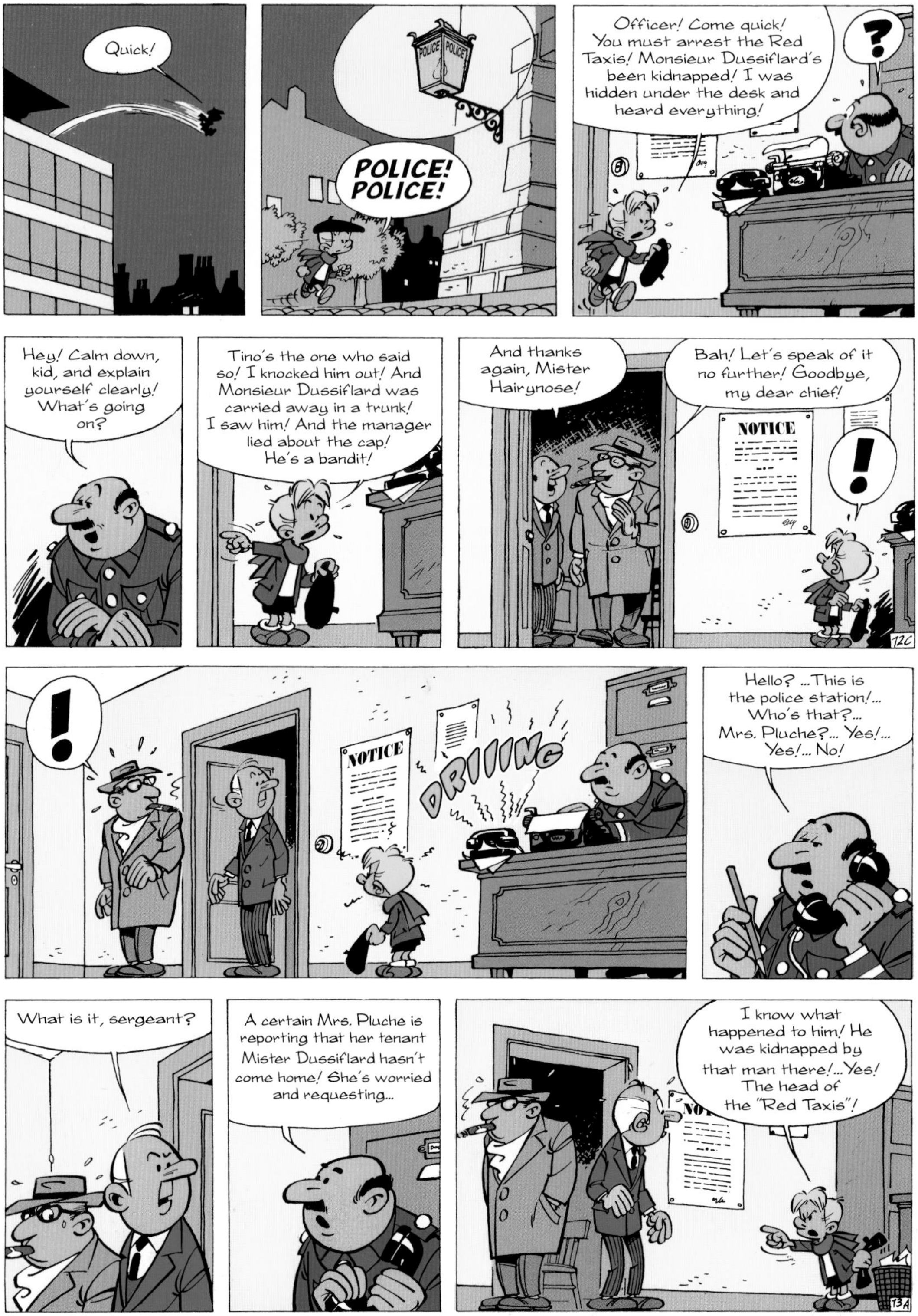

Quick!
POLICE POLICE
POLICE! POLICE!
Officer! Come quick! You must arrest the Red Taxis! Monsieur Dussiflard's been kidnapped! I was hidden under the desk and heard everything!
?
Hey! Calm down, kid, and explain yourself clearly! What's going on?
Tino's the one who said so! I knocked him out! And Monsieur Dussiflard was carried away in a trunk! I saw him! And the manager lied about the cap! He's a bandit!
And thanks again, Mister Hairynose!
Bah! Let's speak of it no further! Goodbye, my dear chief!
NOTICE
!
12C
!
NOTICE
DRIIING
Hello? ...This is the police station!... Who's that?... Mrs. Pluche?... Yes!... Yes!... No!
What is it, sergeant?
A certain Mrs. Pluche is reporting that her tenant Mister Dussiflard hasn't come home! She's worried and requesting...
I know what happened to him! He was kidnapped by that man there!...Yes! The head of the "Red Taxis"!
13A

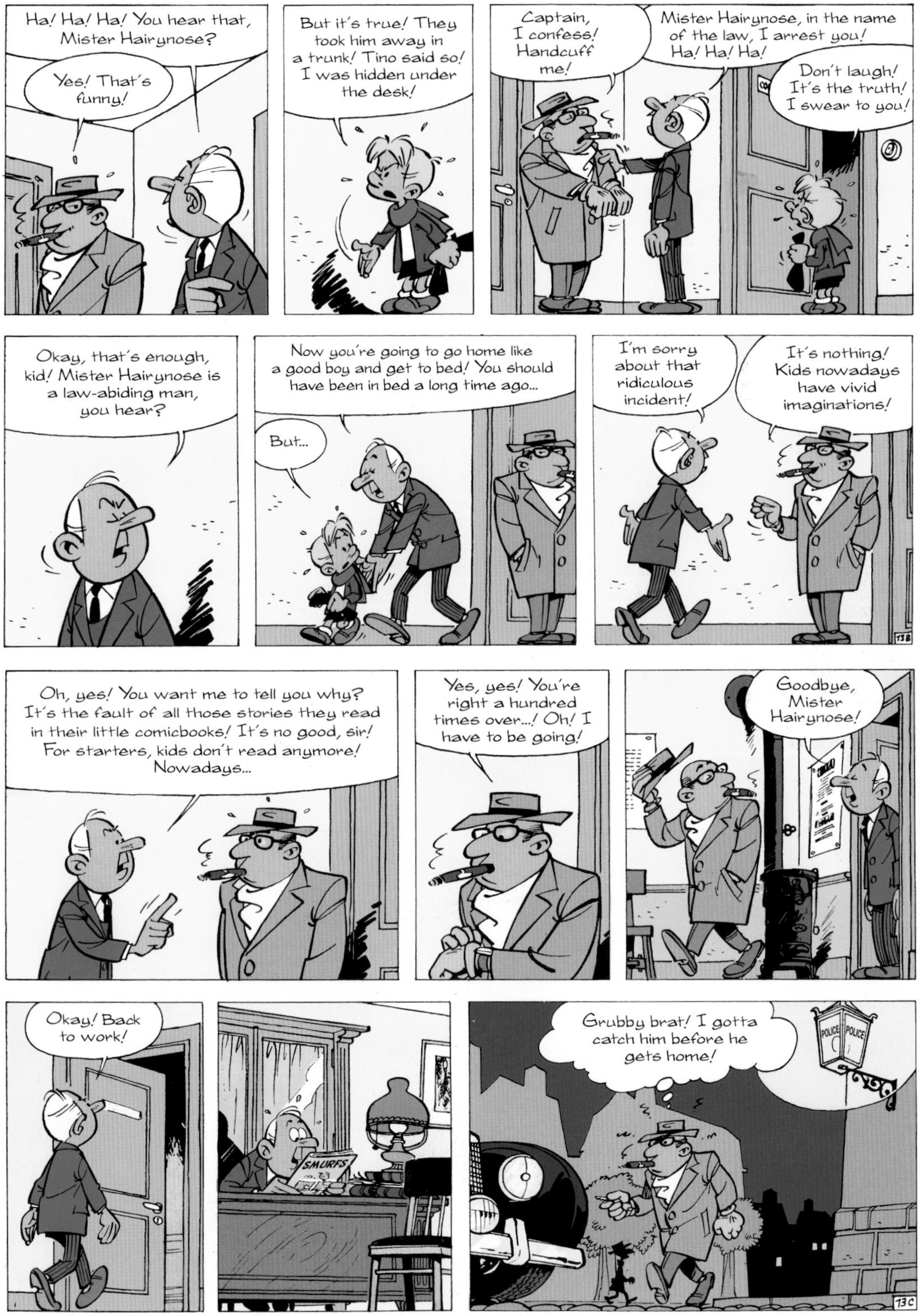
Ha! Ha! Ha! You hear that, Mister Hairynose?
Yes! That's funny!
But it's true! They took him away in a trunk! Tino said so! I was hidden under the desk!
Captain, I confess! Handcuff me!
Mister Hairynose, in the name of the law, I arrest you! Ha! Ha! Ha!
Don't laugh! It's the truth! I swear to you!
Okay, that's enough, kid! Mister Hairynose is a law-abiding man, you hear?
Now you're going to go home like a good boy and get to bed! You should have been in bed a long time ago...
But...
I'm sorry about that ridiculous incident!
It's nothing! Kids nowadays have vivid imaginations!
13B
Oh, yes! You want me to tell you why? It's the fault of all those stories they read in their little comicbooks! It's no good, sir! For starters, kids don't read anymore! Nowadays...
Yes, yes! You're right a hundred times over...! Oh! I have to be going!
Goodbye, Mister Hairynose!
Okay! Back to work!
SMURFS
Grubby brat! I gotta catch him before he gets home!
POLICE
POLICE
13C

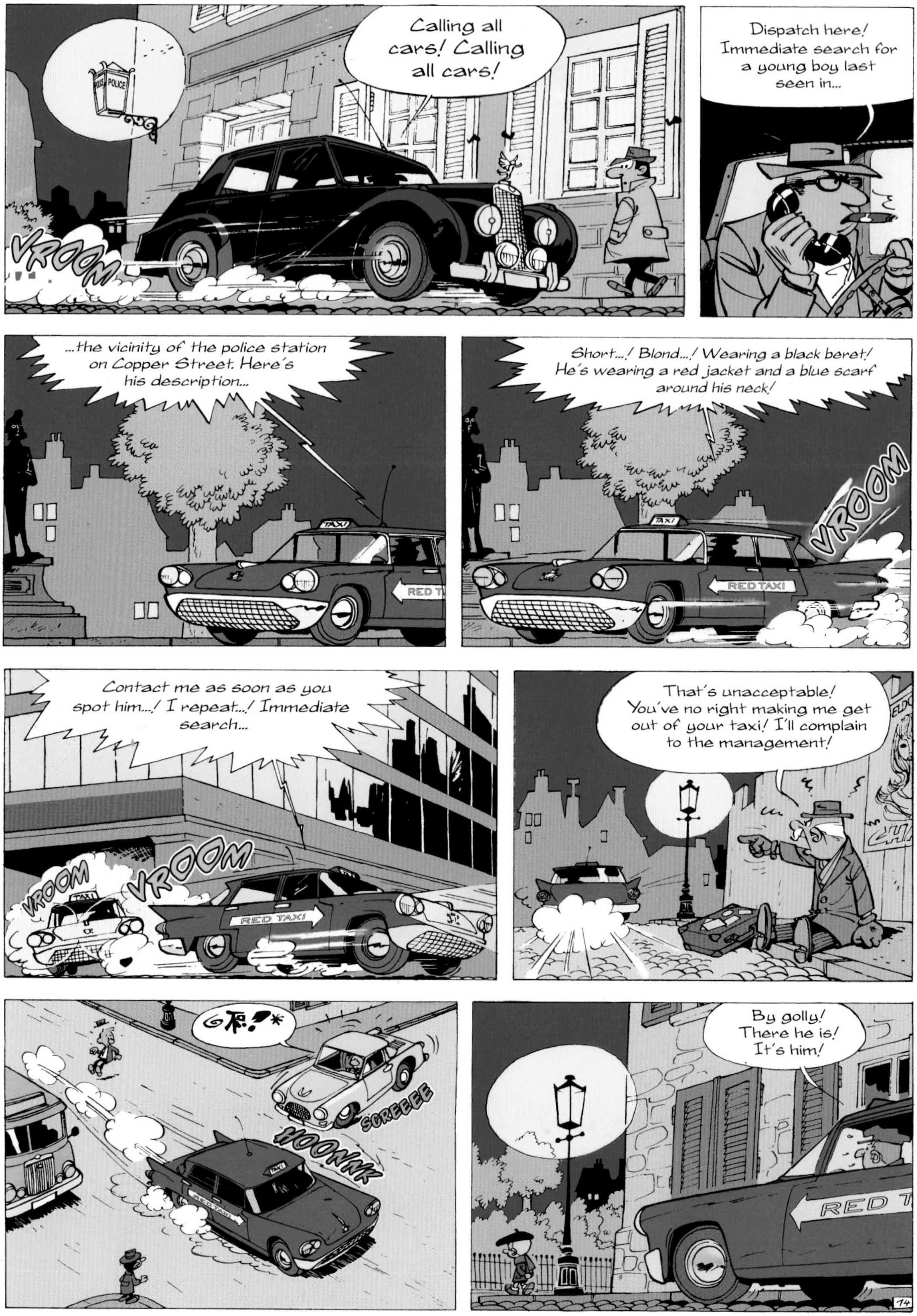
POLICE
Calling all cars! Calling all cars!
VROOM
Dispatch here! Immediate search for a young boy last seen in...
...the vicinity of the police station on Copper Street. Here's his description...
TAXI
RED TAXI
Short...! Blond...! Wearing a black beret! He's wearing a red jacket and a blue scarf around his neck!
VROOM
Contact me as soon as you spot him...! I repeat...! Immediate search...
VROOM
VROOM
RED TAXI
That's unacceptable! You've no right making me get out of your taxi! I'll complain to the management!
SCREEEE
HOONNK
By golly! There he is! It's him!
RED T

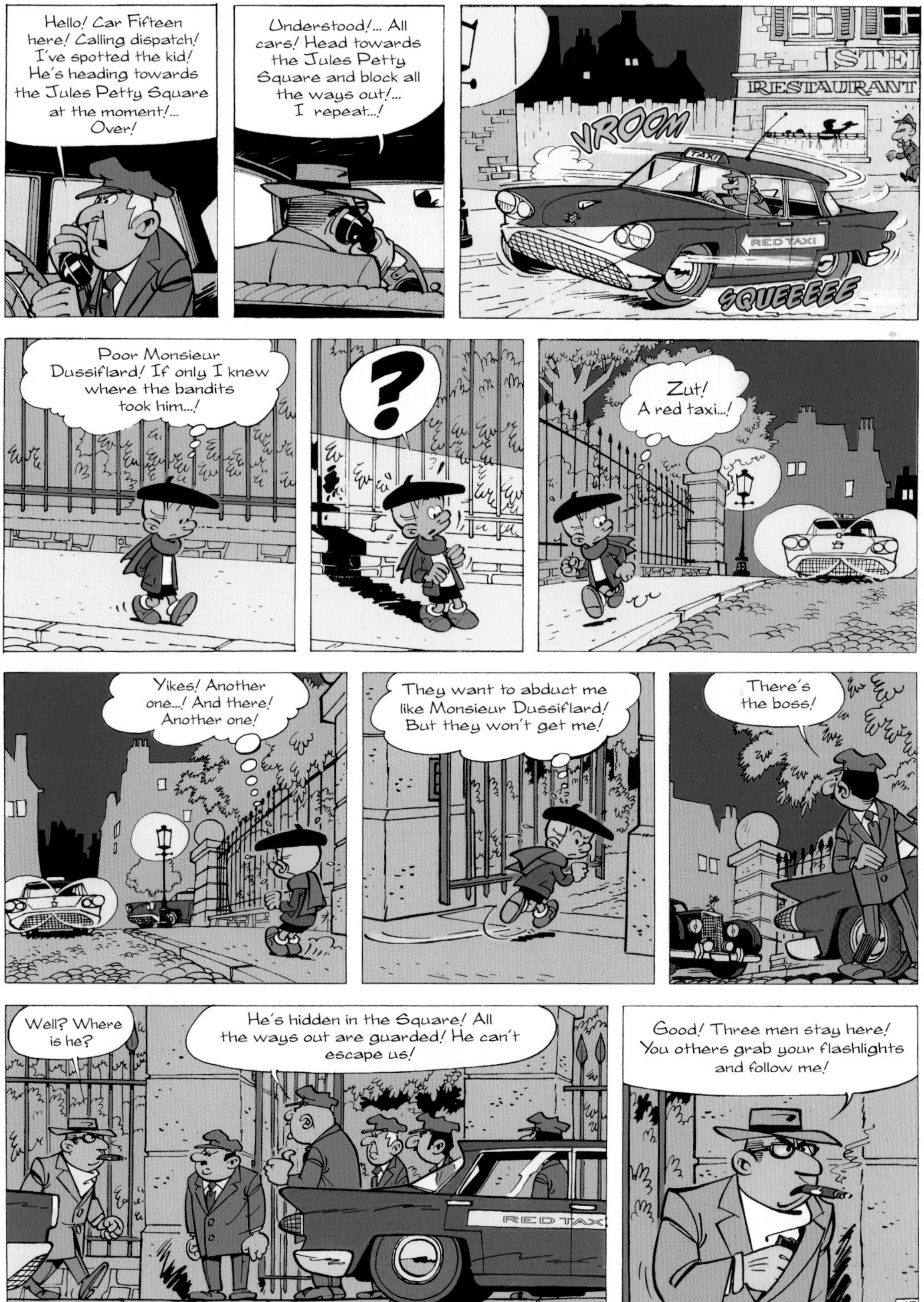
Hello! Car Fifteen here! Calling dispatch! I've spotted the kid! He's heading towards the Jules Petty Square at the moment!... Over!
Understood!... All cars! Head towards the Jules Petty Square and block all the ways out!... I repeat...!
STE
RESTAURANT
VROOM
TAXI
RED TAXI
SQUEEEEEE
Poor Monsieur Dussiflard! If only I knew where the bandits took him...!
?
Zut! A red taxi...!
Yikes! Another one...! And there! Another one!
They want to abduct me like Monsieur Dussiflard! But they won't get me!
There's the boss!
Well? Where is he?
He's hidden in the Square! All the ways out are guarded! He can't escape us!
RED TAX
Good! Three men stay here! You others grab your flashlights and follow me!
15

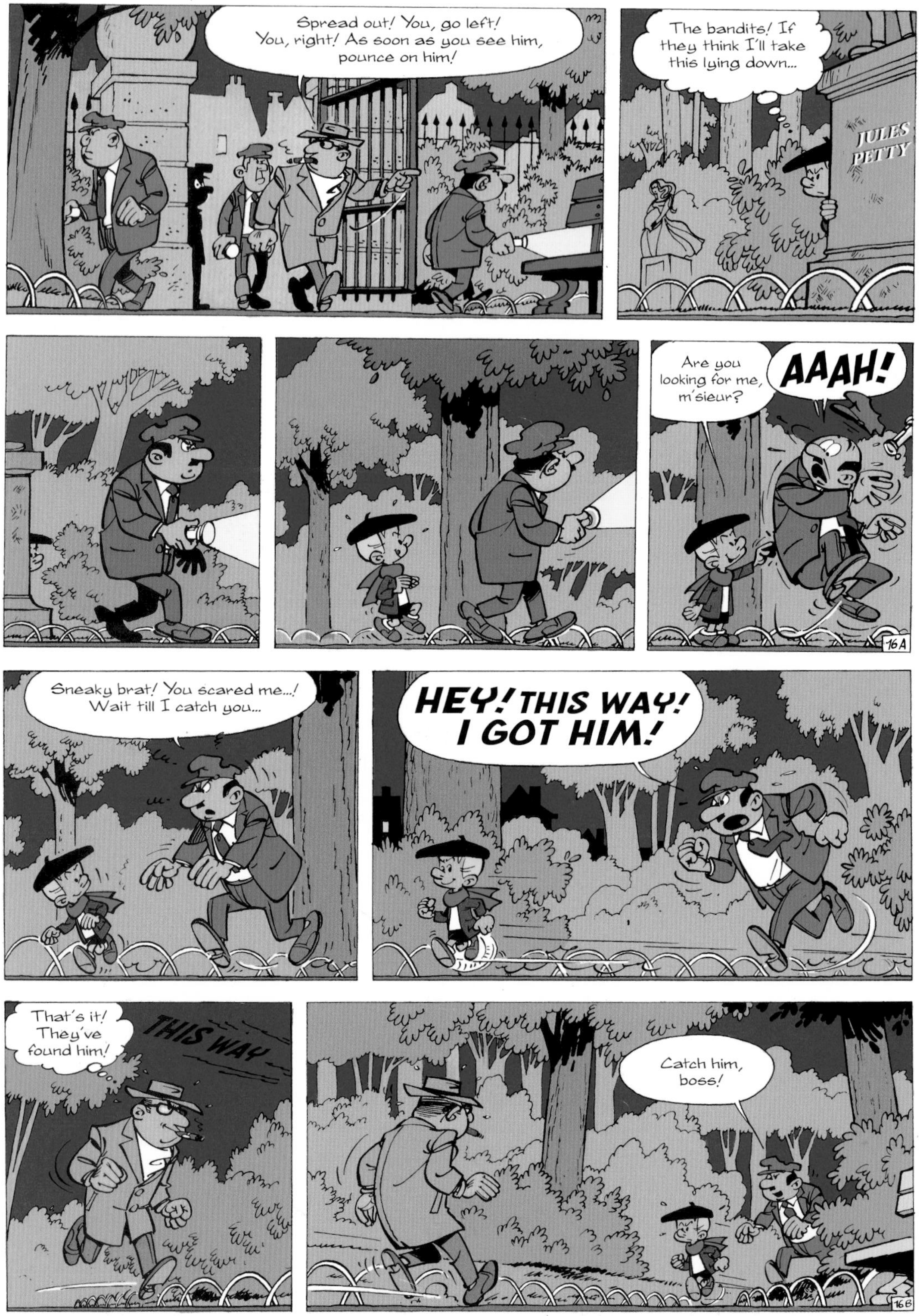
Spread out! You, go left! You, right! As soon as you see him, pounce on him!
The bandits! If they think I'll take this lying down...
JULES PETTY
Are you looking for me, m'sieur?
AAAH!
16 A
Sneaky brat! You scared me...! Wait till I catch you...
HEY! THIS WAY! I GOT HIM!
That's it! They've found him!
THIS WAY
Catch him, boss!
16 B

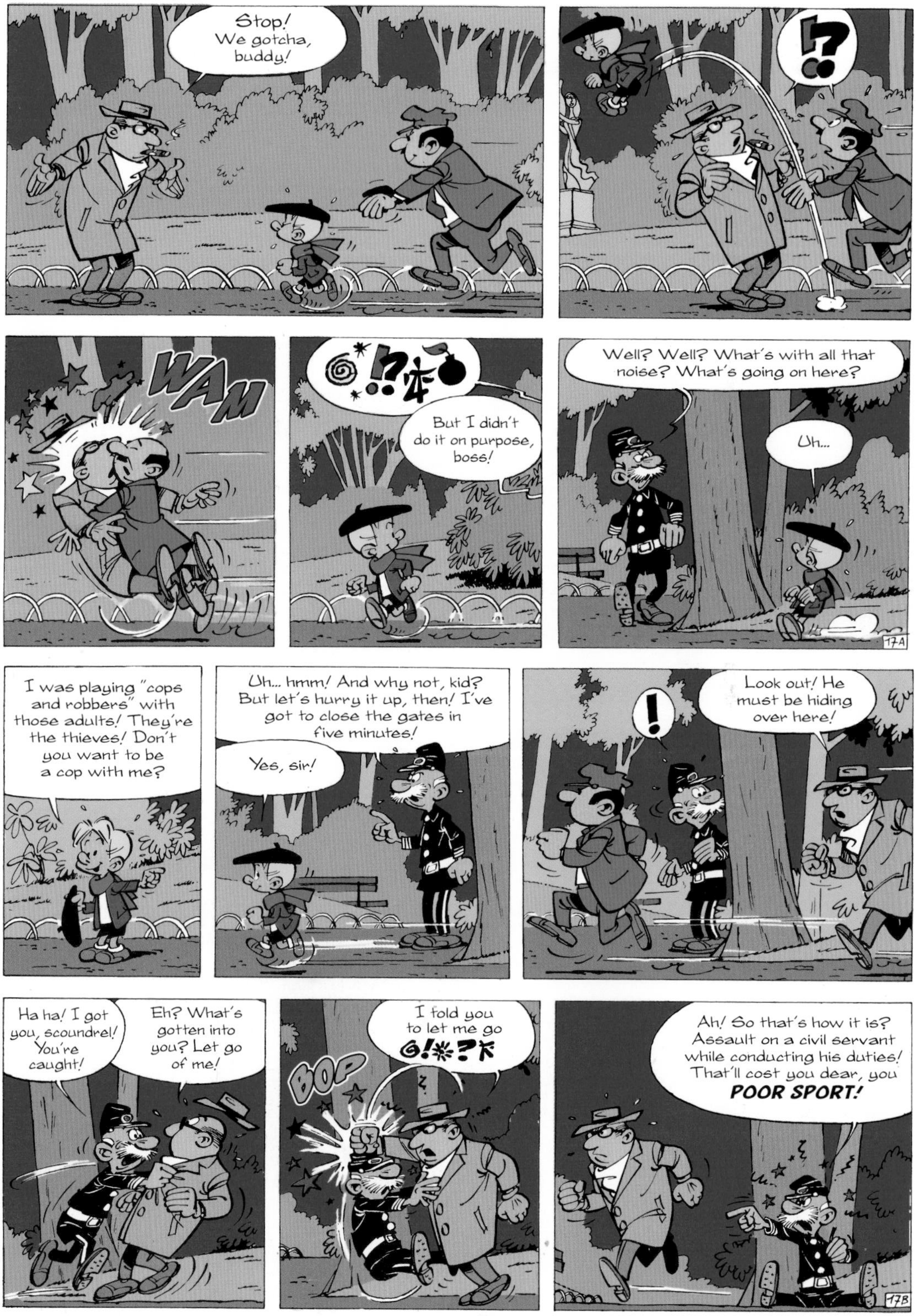
Stop! We gotcha, buddy!
!?
WAM
But I didn't do it on purpose, boss!
Well? Well? What's with all that noise? What's going on here?
Uh...
17A
I was playing "cops and robbers" with those adults! They're the thieves! Don't you want to be a cop with me?
Uh... hmm! And why not, kid? But let's hurry it up, then! I've got to close the gates in five minutes!
Yes, sir!
!
Look out! He must be hiding over here!
Ha ha! I got you, scoundrel! You're caught!
Eh? What's gotten into you? Let go of me!
I told you to let me go
BOP
Ah! So that's how it is? Assault on a civil servant while conducting his duties! That'll cost you dear, you **POOR SPORT!**
17B

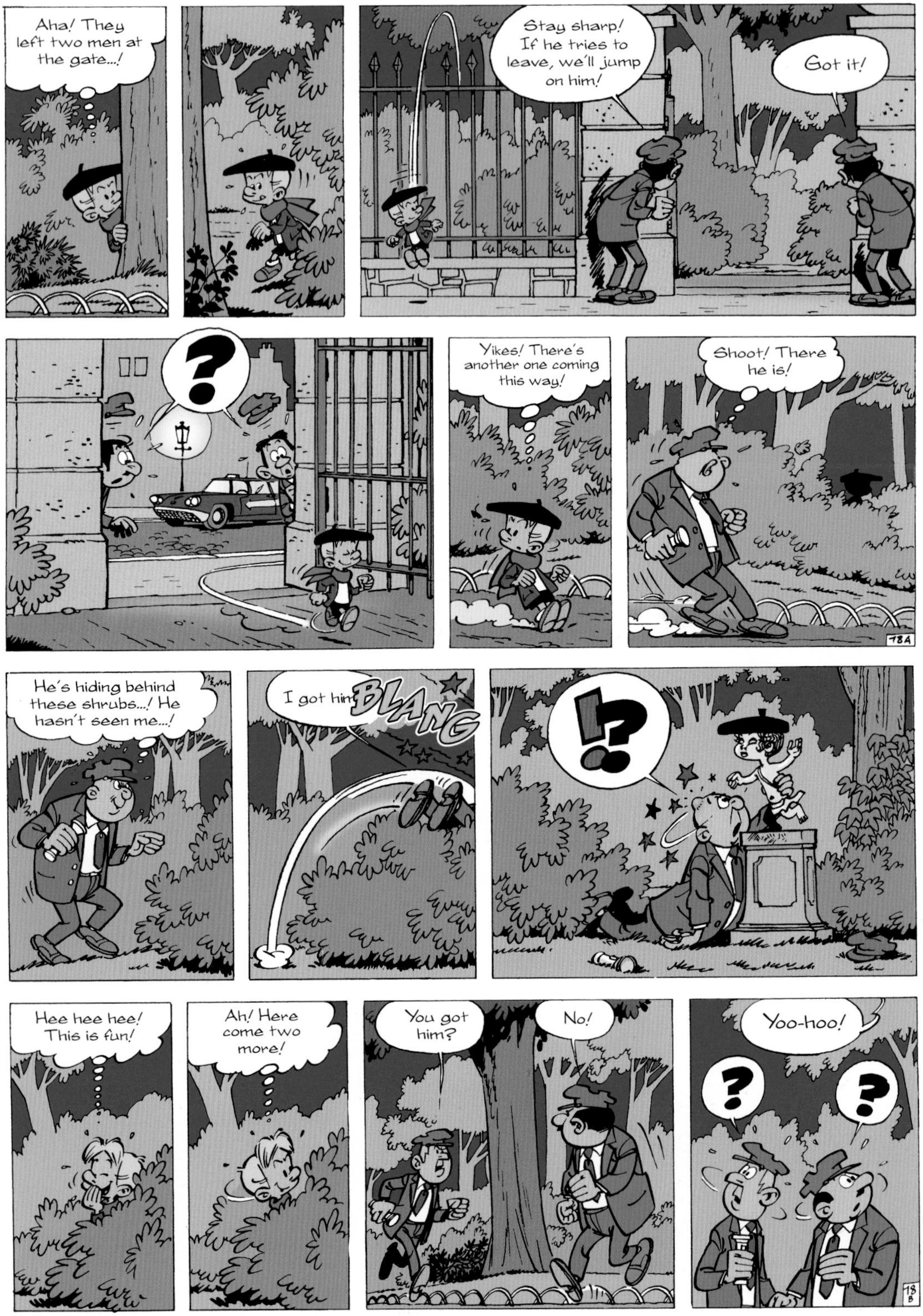
Aha! They left two men at the gate...!
Stay sharp! If he tries to leave, we'll jump on him!
Got it!
?
Yikes! There's another one coming this way!
Shoot! There he is!
18A
He's hiding behind these shrubs...! He hasn't seen me...!
I got him
BLANG
!?
Hee hee hee! This is fun!
Ah! Here come two more!
You got him?
No!
Yoo-hoo!
?
?
18B

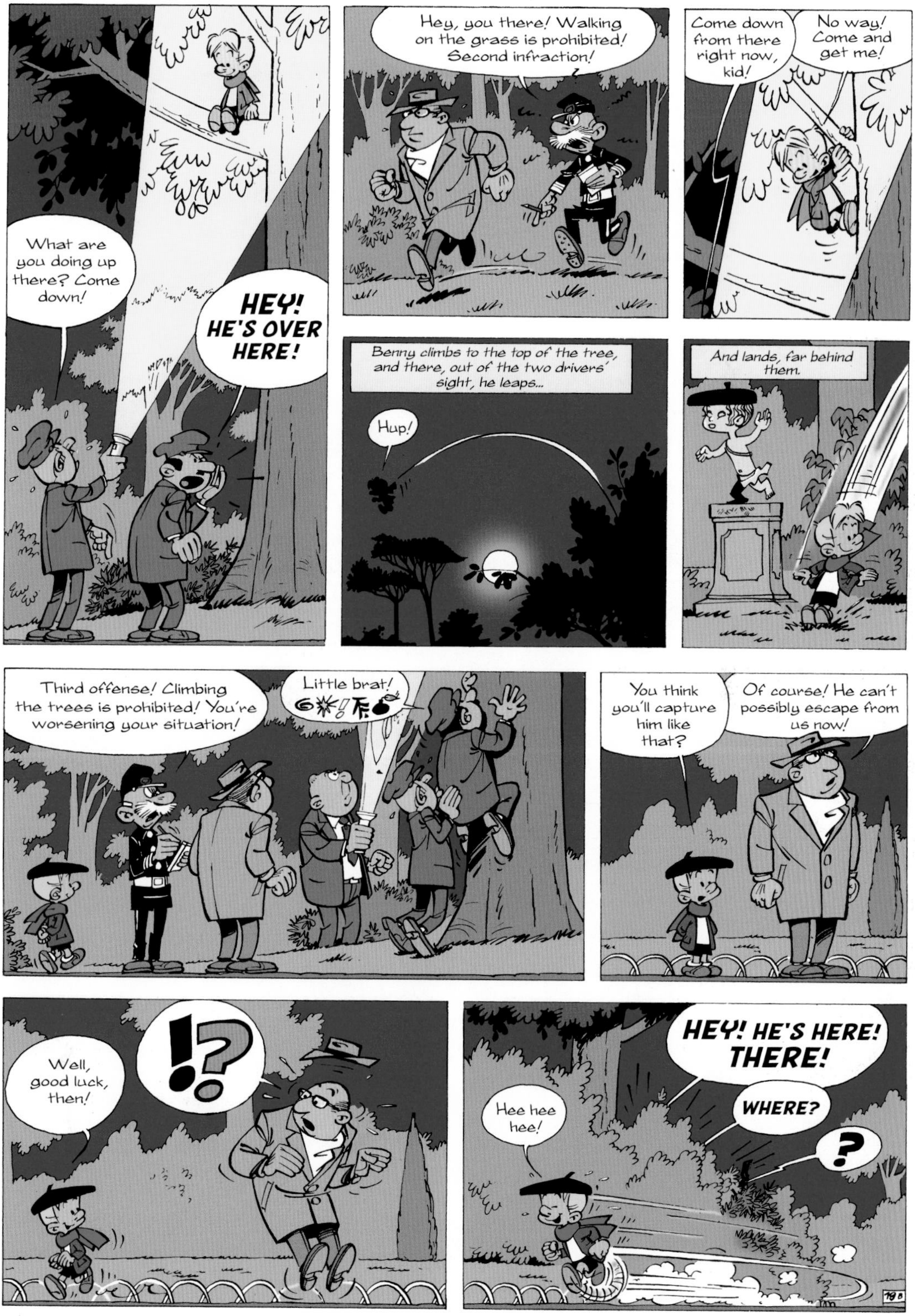

What are you doing up there? Come down!
HEY! HE'S OVER HERE!
Hey, you there! Walking on the grass is prohibited! Second infraction!
Come down from there right now, kid!
No way! Come and get me!
Benny climbs to the top of the tree, and there, out of the two drivers' sight, he leaps...
Hup!
And lands, far behind them.
Third offense! Climbing the trees is prohibited! You're worsening your situation!
Little brat!
You think you'll capture him like that?
Of course! He can't possibly escape from us now!
Well, good luck, then!
!?
HEY! HE'S HERE! THERE!
Hee hee hee!
WHERE?
?

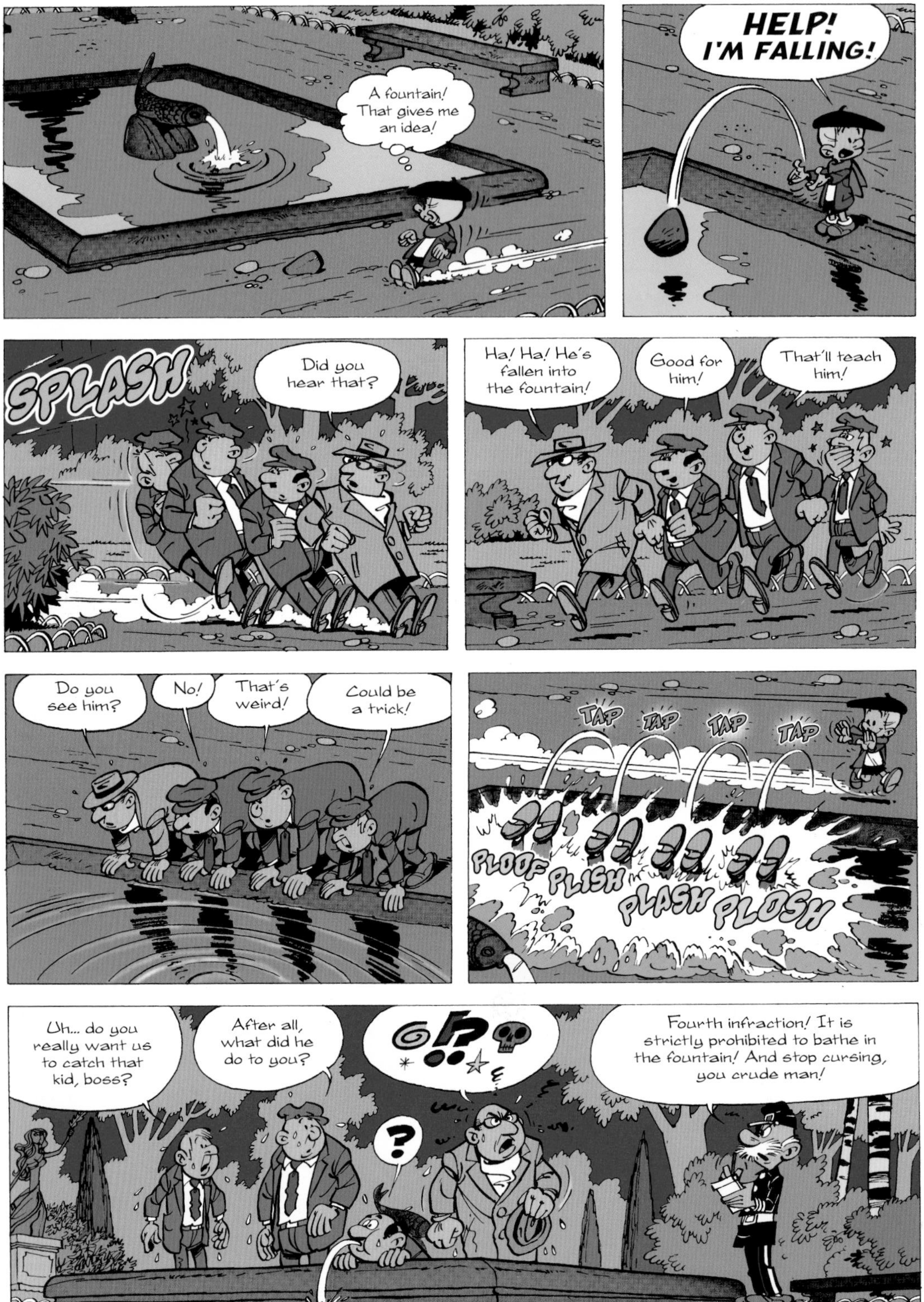
A fountain! That gives me an idea!
HELP! I'M FALLING!
SPLASH
Did you hear that?
Ha! Ha! He's fallen into the fountain!
Good for him!
That'll teach him!
Do you see him?
No!
That's weird!
Could be a trick!
TAP
TAP
TAP
TAP
PLOOF
PLISH
PLASH
PLOSH
Uh... do you really want us to catch that kid, boss?
After all, what did he do to you?
?
Fourth infraction! It is strictly prohibited to bathe in the fountain! And stop cursing, you crude man!

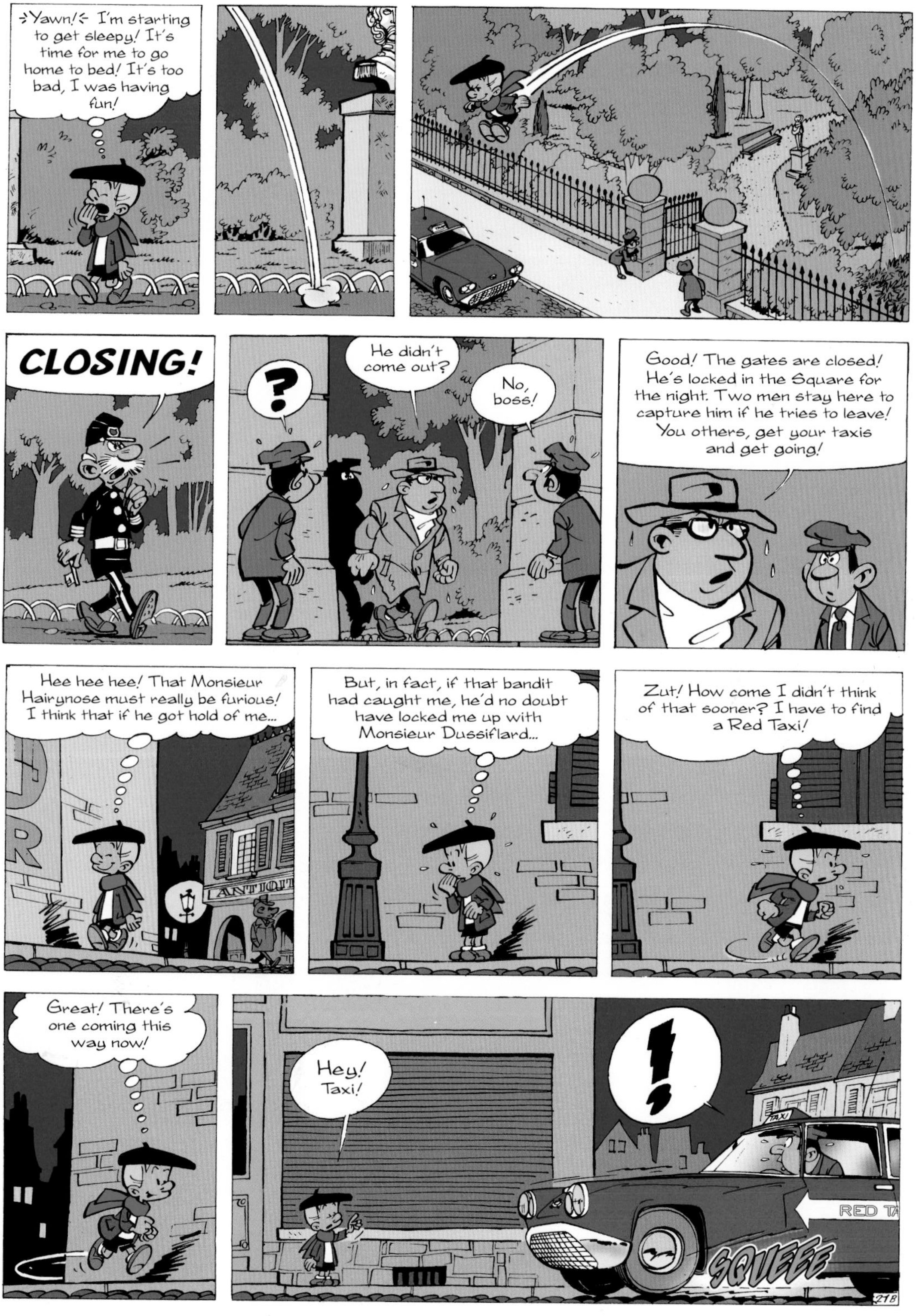

Yawn! I'm starting to get sleepy! It's time for me to go home to bed! It's too bad, I was having fun!
CLOSING!
?
He didn't come out?
No, boss!
Good! The gates are closed! He's locked in the Square for the night. Two men stay here to capture him if he tries to leave! You others, get your taxis and get going!
Hee hee hee! That Monsieur Hairynose must really be furious! I think that if he got hold of me...
But, in fact, if that bandit had caught me, he'd no doubt have locked me up with Monsieur Dussiflard...
Zut! How come I didn't think of that sooner? I have to find a Red Taxi!
Great! There's one coming this way now!
Hey! Taxi!
!
TAXI
RED TA
SQUEEE

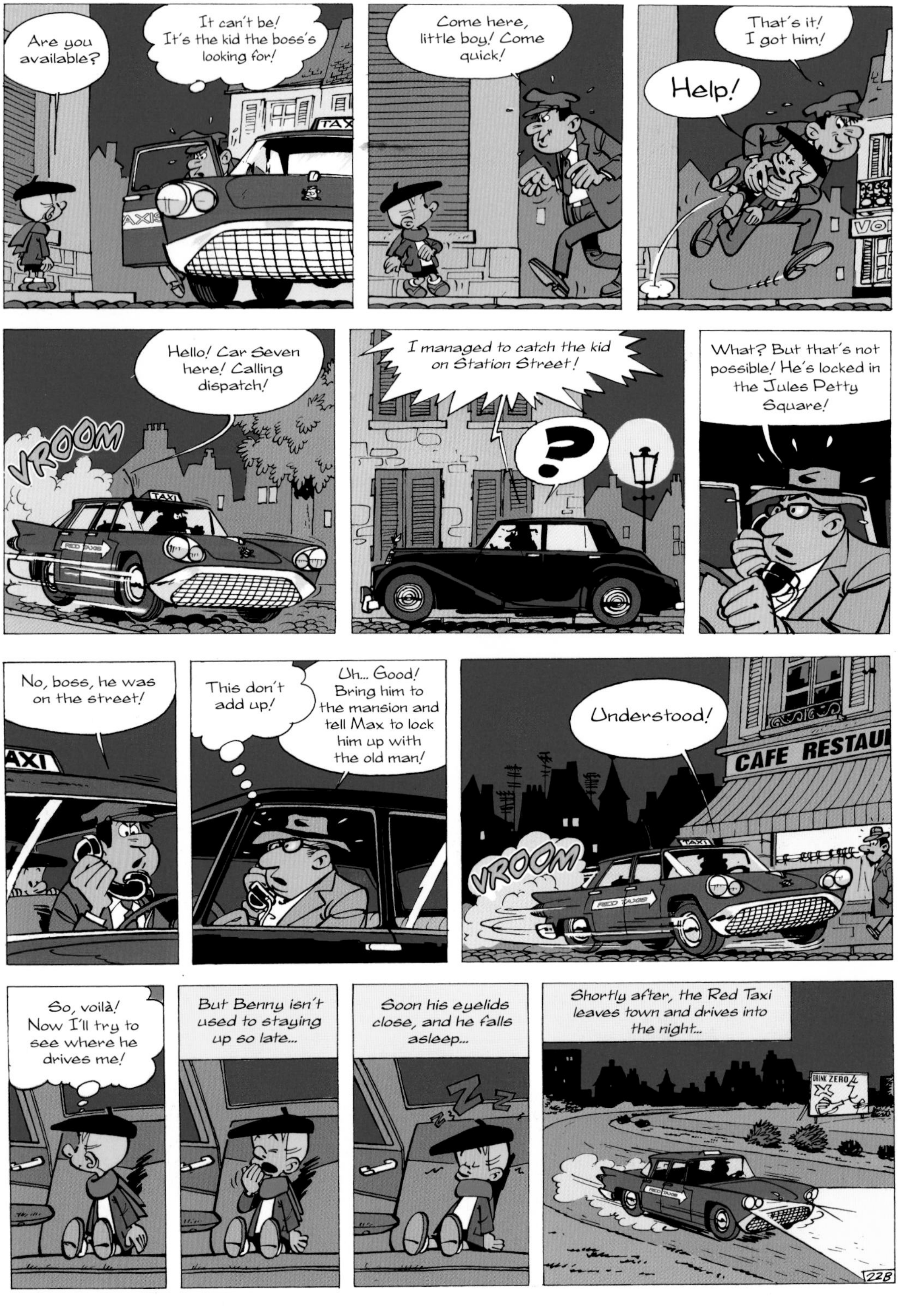
Are you available?
It can't be! It's the kid the boss's looking for!
TAXI
Come here, little boy! Come quick!
That's it! I got him!
Help!
Hello! Car Seven here! Calling dispatch!
VROOM
TAXI
I managed to catch the kid on Station Street!
?
What? But that's not possible! He's locked in the Jules Petty Square!
No, boss, he was on the street!
TAXI
This don't add up!
Uh... Good! Bring him to the mansion and tell Max to lock him up with the old man!
Understood!
CAFE RESTAU
VROOM
So, voilà! Now I'll try to see where he drives me!
But Benny isn't used to staying up so late...
Soon his eyelids close, and he falls asleep...
Z Z Z
Shortly after, the Red Taxi leaves town and drives into the night...
DRINK ZERO
22B

The next morning...

Ah! Are you awake, Benny?

Monsieur Dussiflard!

Poor little friend! So, those bandits got you, too?

Yes! But I let myself get caught on purpose! In order to be able to come rescue you!

What...? But, Benny...

Don't worry! We're going to escape!

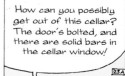

How can you possibly get out of this cellar? The door's bolted, and there are solid bars in the cellar window!

Well, we'll just have to remove them!

That's impossible! I tried all night! We'd need tools!

But no....!

Monsieur Dussiflard, I have to confide my secret to you! Don't repeat it to anyone, but *I AM STRONG!*

Why, yes, Benny! And if you eat your brussel sprouts, you'll get even stronger!

You don't understand me! I'm **INCREDIBLY STRONG!**

Yes! Yes! I'm sure...

You don't believe me, eh? Well, then you're going to see what I can do!

Right!

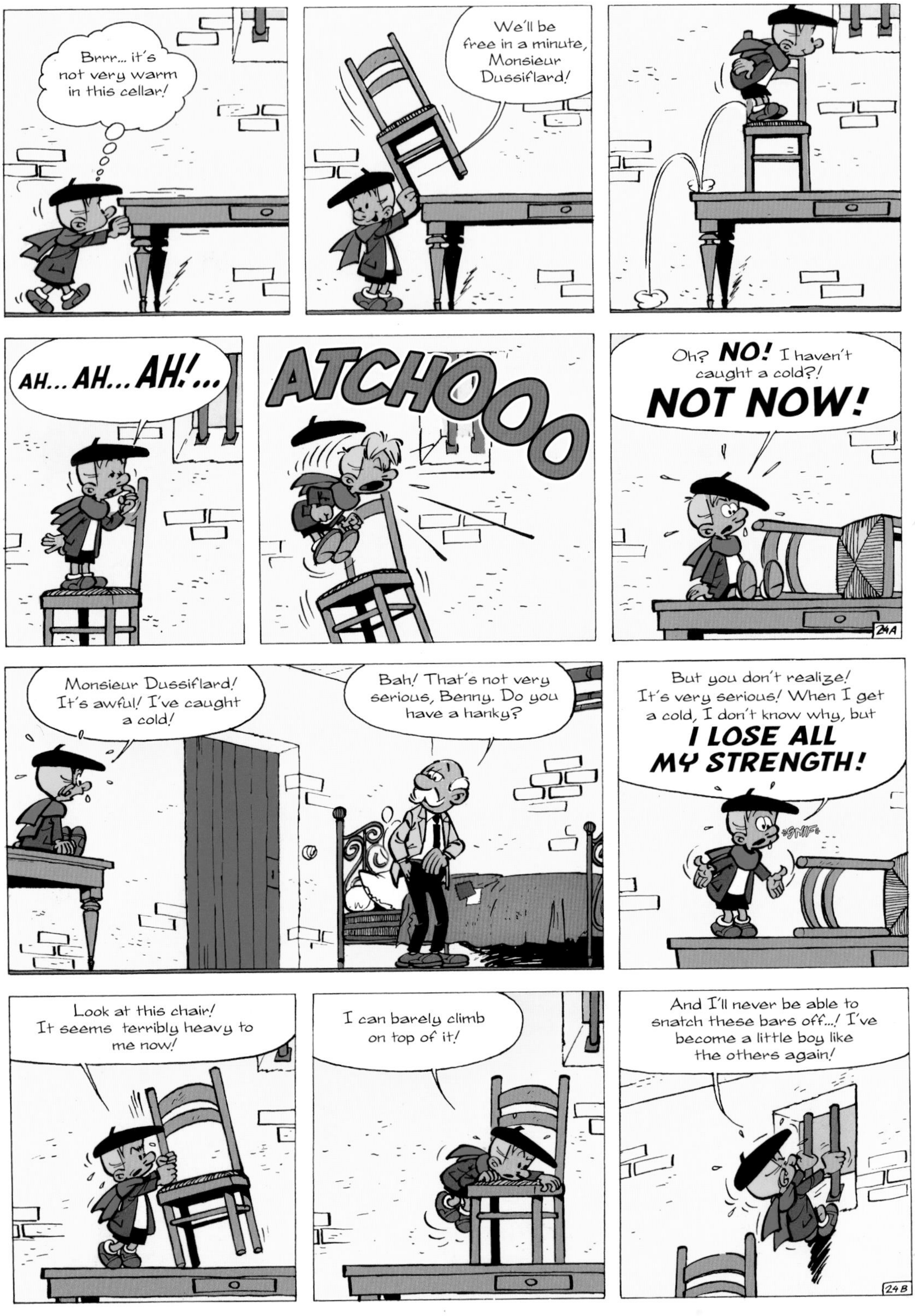
Brrr... it's not very warm in this cellar!
We'll be free in a minute, Monsieur Dussiflard!
AH... AH... AH!...
ATCHOOO
Oh? NO! I haven't caught a cold?! NOT NOW!
24A
Monsieur Dussiflard! It's awful! I've caught a cold!
Bah! That's not very serious, Benny. Do you have a hanky?
But you don't realize! It's very serious! When I get a cold, I don't know why, but I LOSE ALL MY STRENGTH!
SNIF
Look at this chair! It seems terribly heavy to me now!
I can barely climb on top of it!
And I'll never be able to snatch these bars off...! I've become a little boy like the others again!
24B

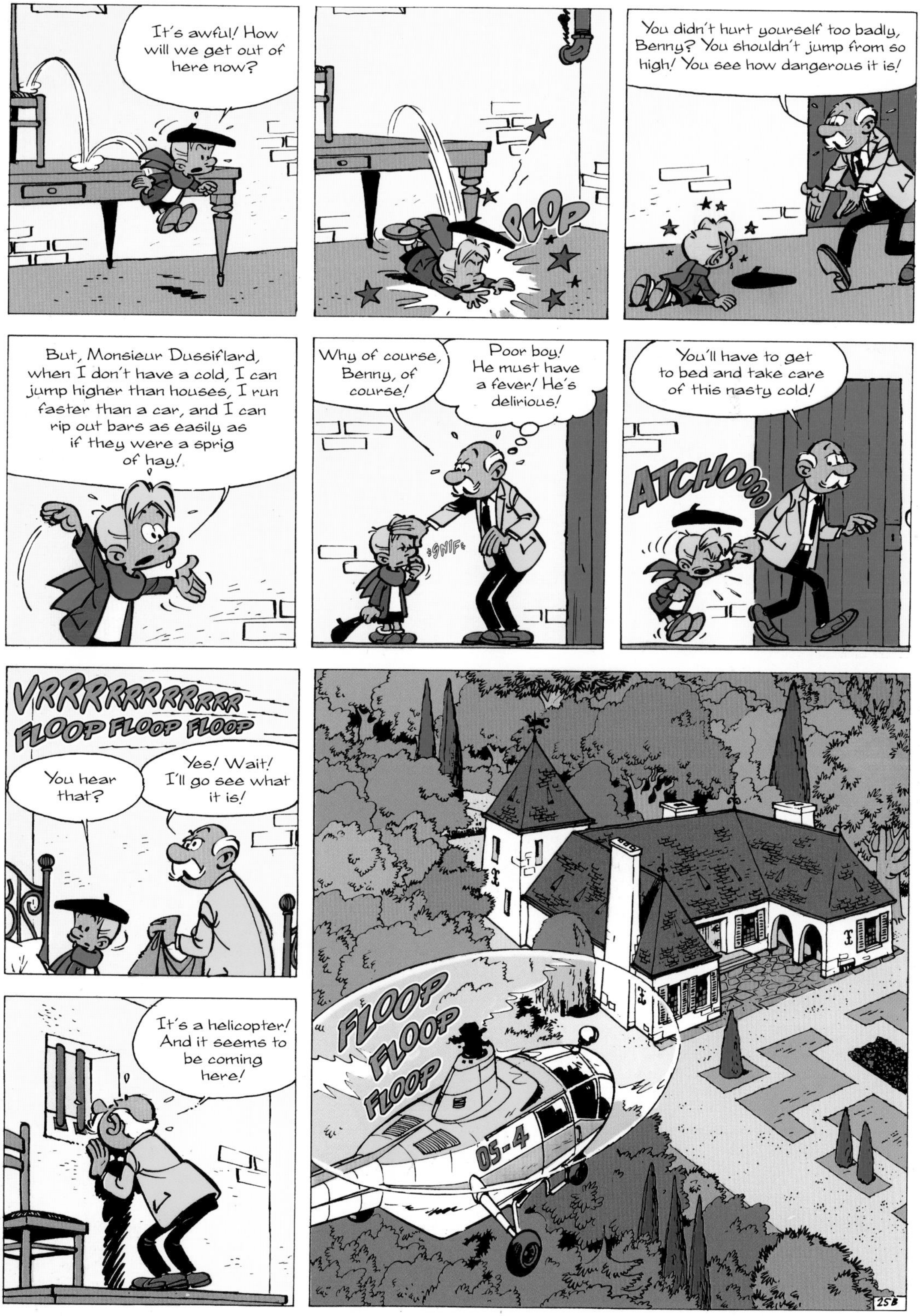

It's awful! How will we get out of here now?
PLOP
You didn't hurt yourself too badly, Benny? You shouldn't jump from so high! You see how dangerous it is!
But, Monsieur Dussiflard, when I don't have a cold, I can jump higher than houses, I run faster than a car, and I can rip out bars as easily as if they were a sprig of hay!
Why of course, Benny, of course!
Poor boy! He must have a fever! He's delirious!
SNIF
You'll have to get to bed and take care of this nasty cold!
ATCHOOOO
VRRRRRRRRRRR
FLOOP FLOOP FLOOP
You hear that?
Yes! Wait! I'll go see what it is!
It's a helicopter! And it seems to be coming here!
FLOOP FLOOP FLOOP
OS-4
25B

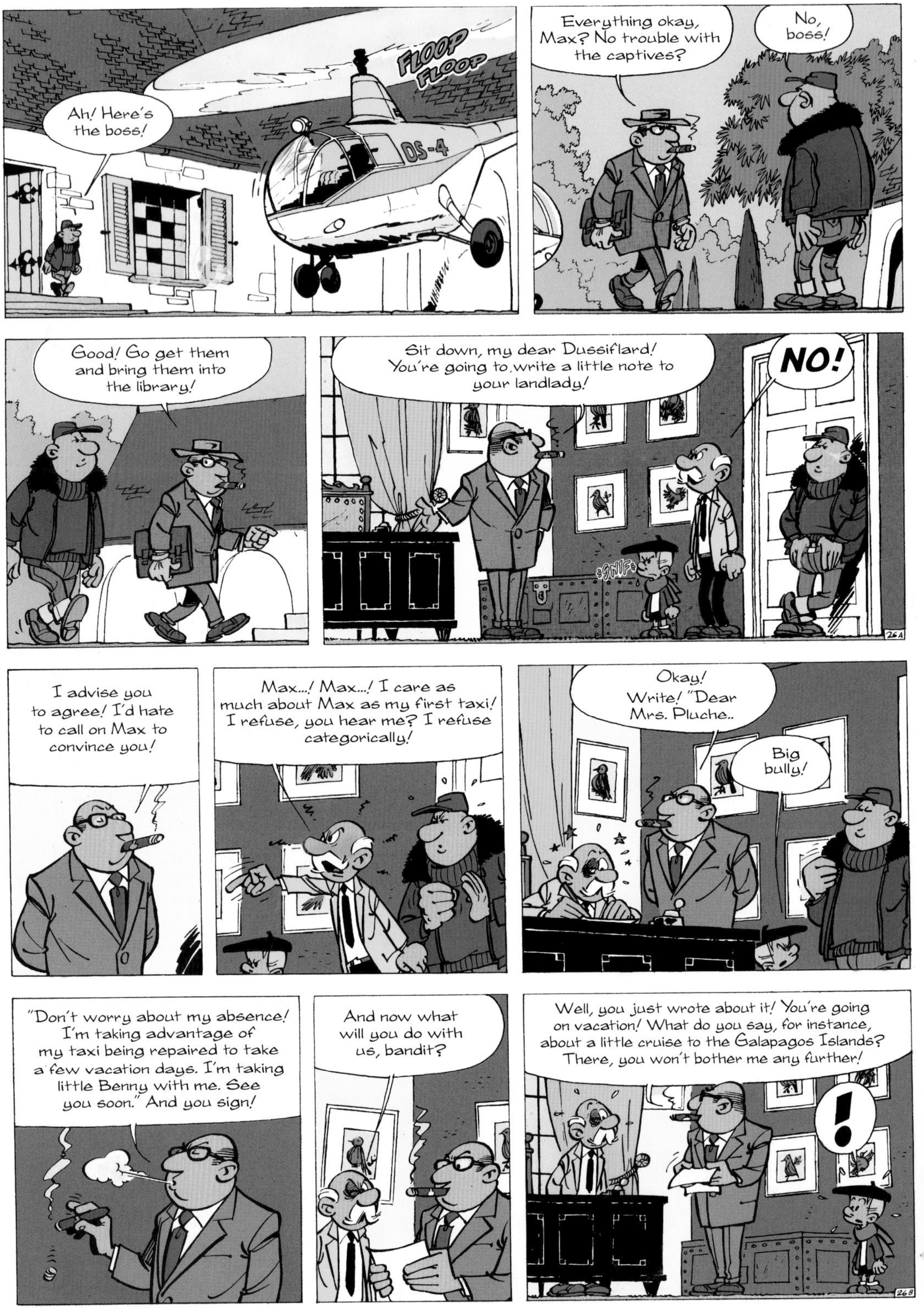
FLOOP FLOOP
Ah! Here's the boss!
OS-4
Everything okay, Max? No trouble with the captives?
No, boss!
Good! Go get them and bring them into the library!
Sit down, my dear Dussiflard! You're going to write a little note to your landlady!
NO!
SNIF
26A
I advise you to agree! I'd hate to call on Max to convince you!
Max...! Max...! I care as much about Max as my first taxi! I refuse, you hear me? I refuse categorically!
Okay! Write! "Dear Mrs. Pluche..
Big bully!
"Don't worry about my absence! I'm taking advantage of my taxi being repaired to take a few vacation days. I'm taking little Benny with me. See you soon." And you sign!
And now what will you do with us, bandit?
Well, you just wrote about it! You're going on vacation! What do you say, for instance, about a little cruise to the Galapagos Islands? There, you won't bother me any further!
!
26B

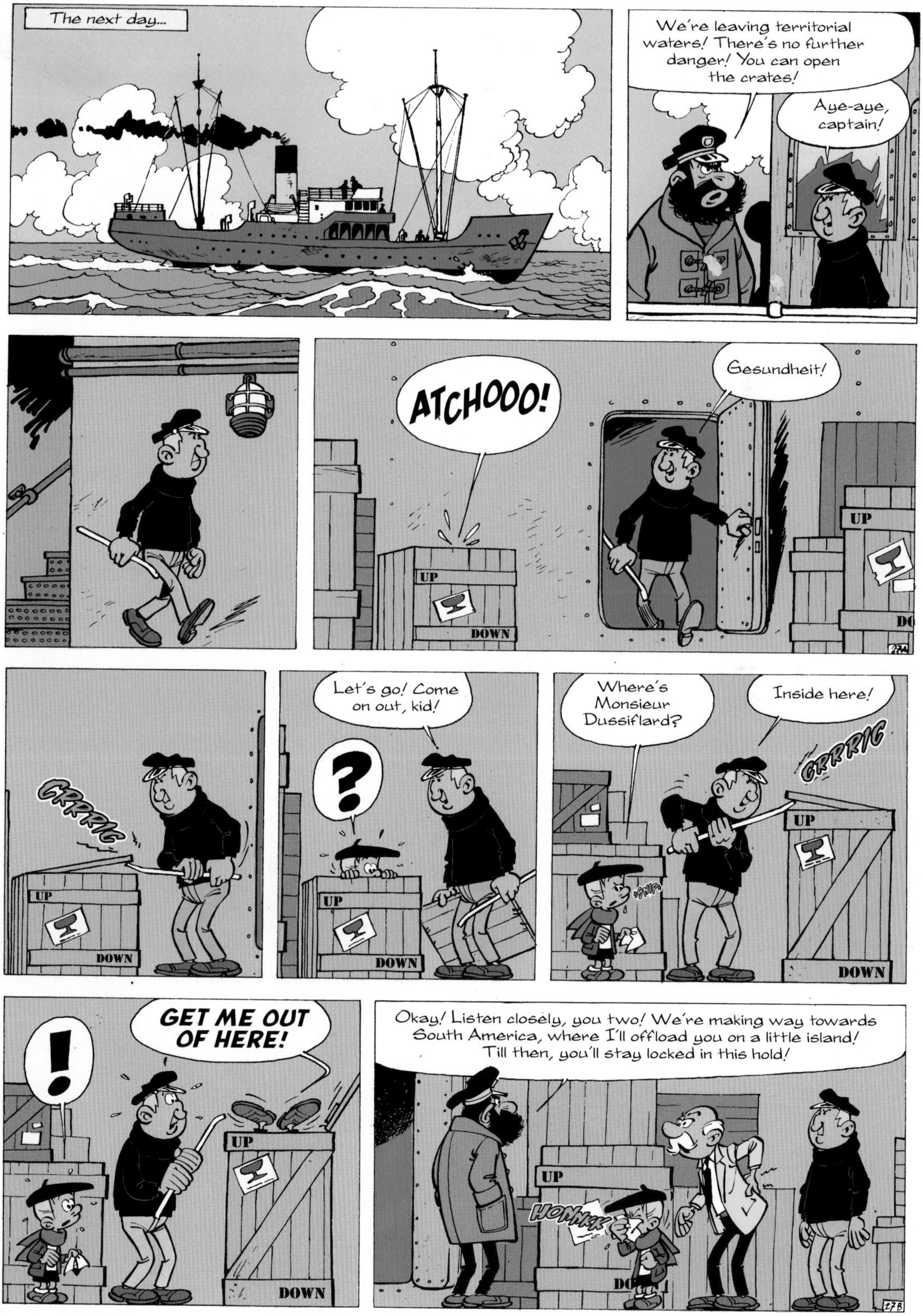

The next day...
We're leaving territorial waters! There's no further danger! You can open the crates!
Aye-aye, captain!
ATCHOOO!
Gesundheit!
UP
DOWN
CRRRIG
Let's go! Come on out, kid!
?
Where's Monsieur Dussiflard?
Inside here!
CRRRIG
SNIFF
GET ME OUT OF HERE!
!
Okay! Listen closely, you two! We're making way towards South America, where I'll offload you on a little island! Till then, you'll stay locked in this hold!
HONKK

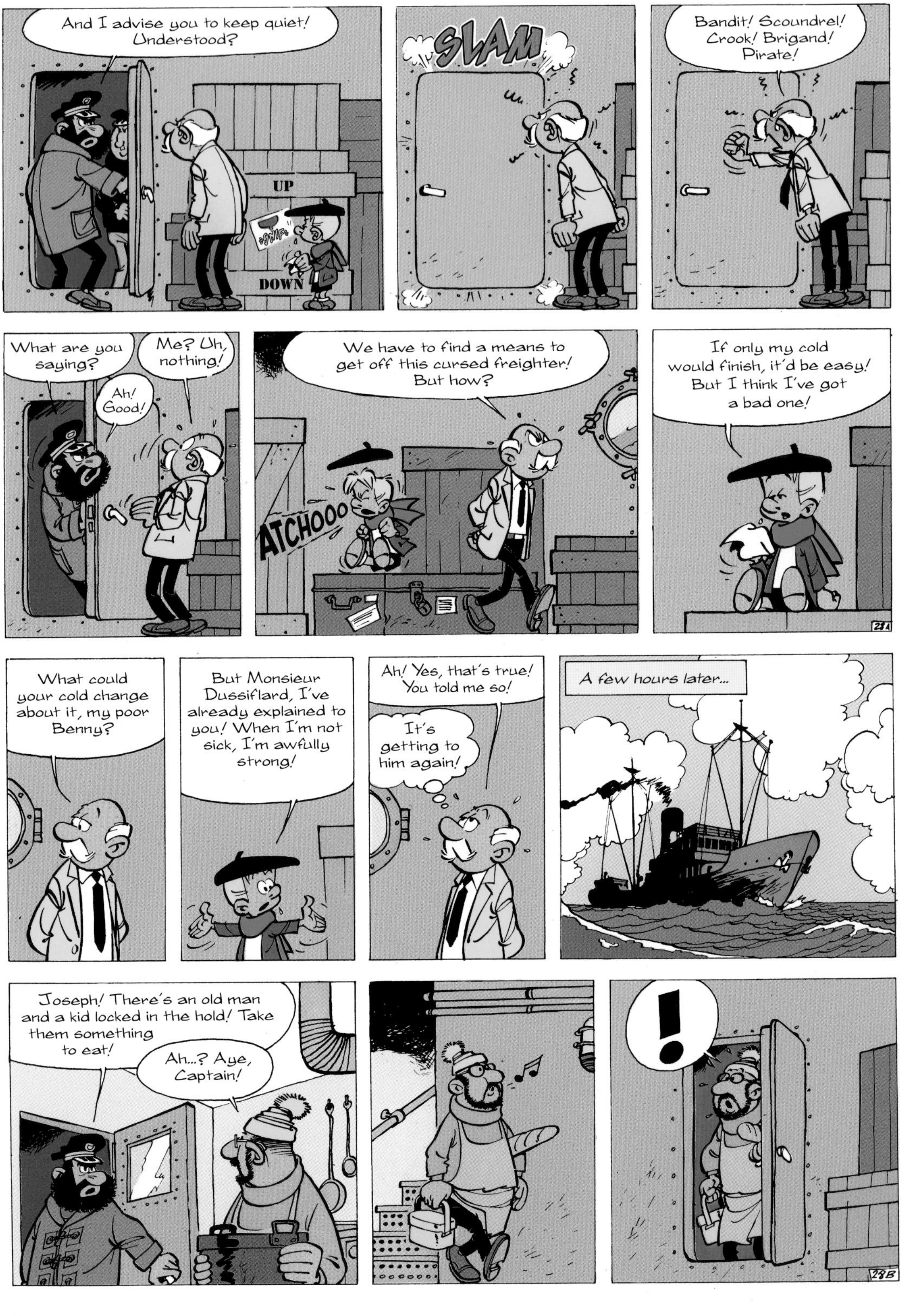
And I advise you to keep quiet! Understood?
UP
SNIF
DOWN
SLAM
Bandit! Scoundrel! Crook! Brigand! Pirate!
What are you saying?
Me? Uh, nothing!
Ah! Good!
We have to find a means to get off this cursed freighter! But how?
ATCHOOO
If only my cold would finish, it'd be easy! But I think I've got a bad one!
28A
What could your cold change about it, my poor Benny?
But Monsieur Dussiflard, I've already explained to you! When I'm not sick, I'm awfully strong!
Ah! Yes, that's true! You told me so!
It's getting to him again!
A few hours later...
Joseph! There's an old man and a kid locked in the hold! Take them something to eat!
Ah...? Aye, Captain!
!
28B

JOSEPH!

JULES!

?

My old friend Joseph! I never expected to find you here...

Tell me about it! Ha! Ha! Ha! We haven't seen each other in years!

Look, Benny! It's Joseph, my old Army buddy! We were in the War together!

Ah, yes! The good ol' days!

But, hey, what happened? Why are you locked in this hold?

Oh! It's quite the tale!

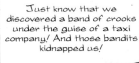

Just know that we discovered a band of crooks under the guise of a taxi company! And those bandits kidnapped us!

To get rid of us, they forcibly boarded us onto this freighter, whose captain was paid to unload us on the Galapagos Islands!

Oh, my...! Oh, me, oh, my...!

Listen, Joseph! You have to help us off this boat as fast as possible!

What? But we're on the open seas! That's madness! We're miles from the coast!

Too bad! I'll take the risk! Can you get us a lifeboat?

Uh, I don't know...! I'll try...!

Careful! Someone's coming!

I'll see what I can do for you! I'll keep you informed!

You're still here?

No! Uh... yes! I... I'm done, captain!

GLIK GLAK

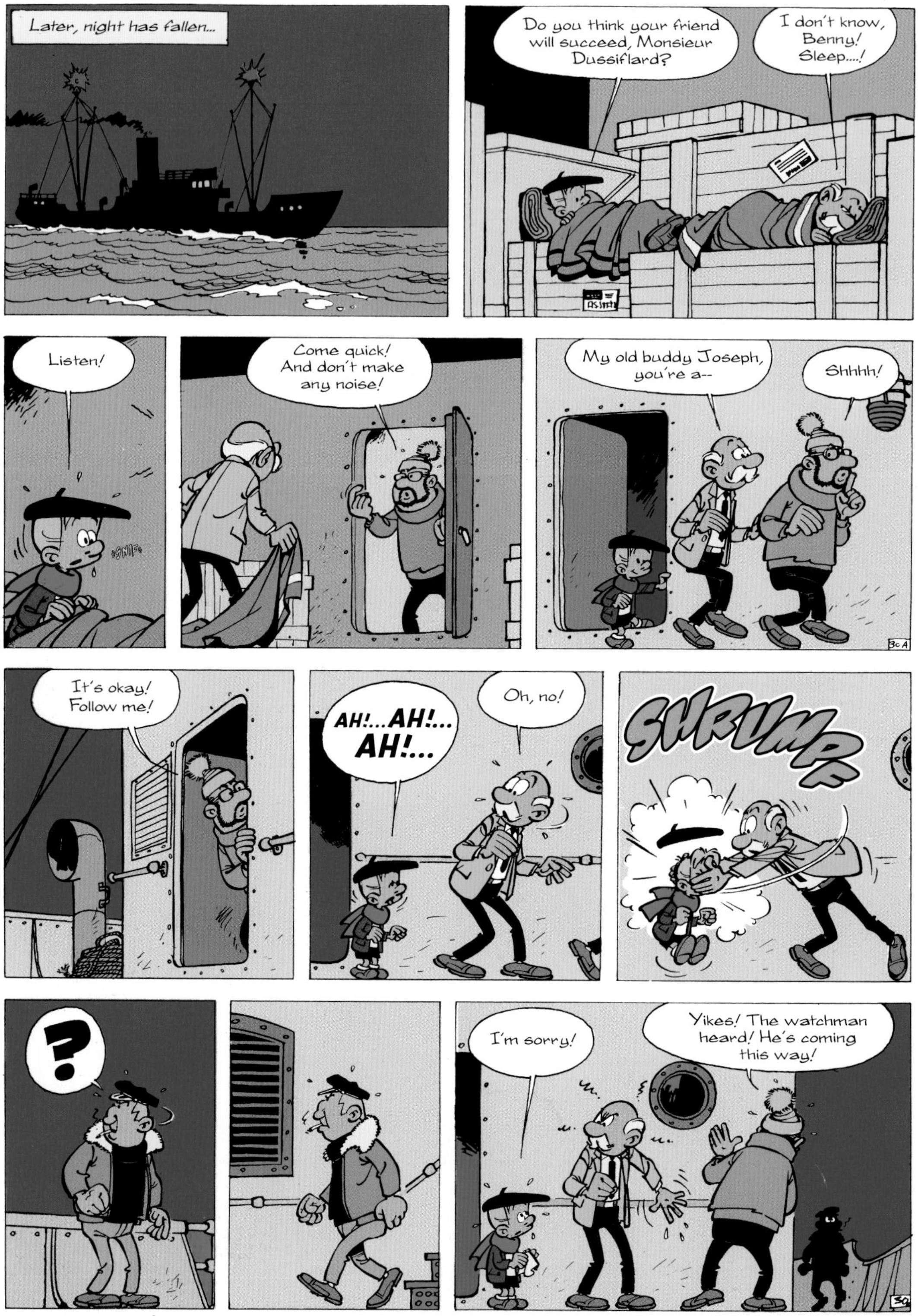
Later, night has fallen...
Do you think your friend will succeed, Monsieur Dussiflard?
I don't know, Benny! Sleep....!
Listen!
SNIF
Come quick! And don't make any noise!
My old buddy Joseph, you're a--
Shhhh!
It's okay! Follow me!
AH!...AH!... AH!...
Oh, no!
SHRUMPF
?
I'm sorry!
Yikes! The watchman heard! He's coming this way!

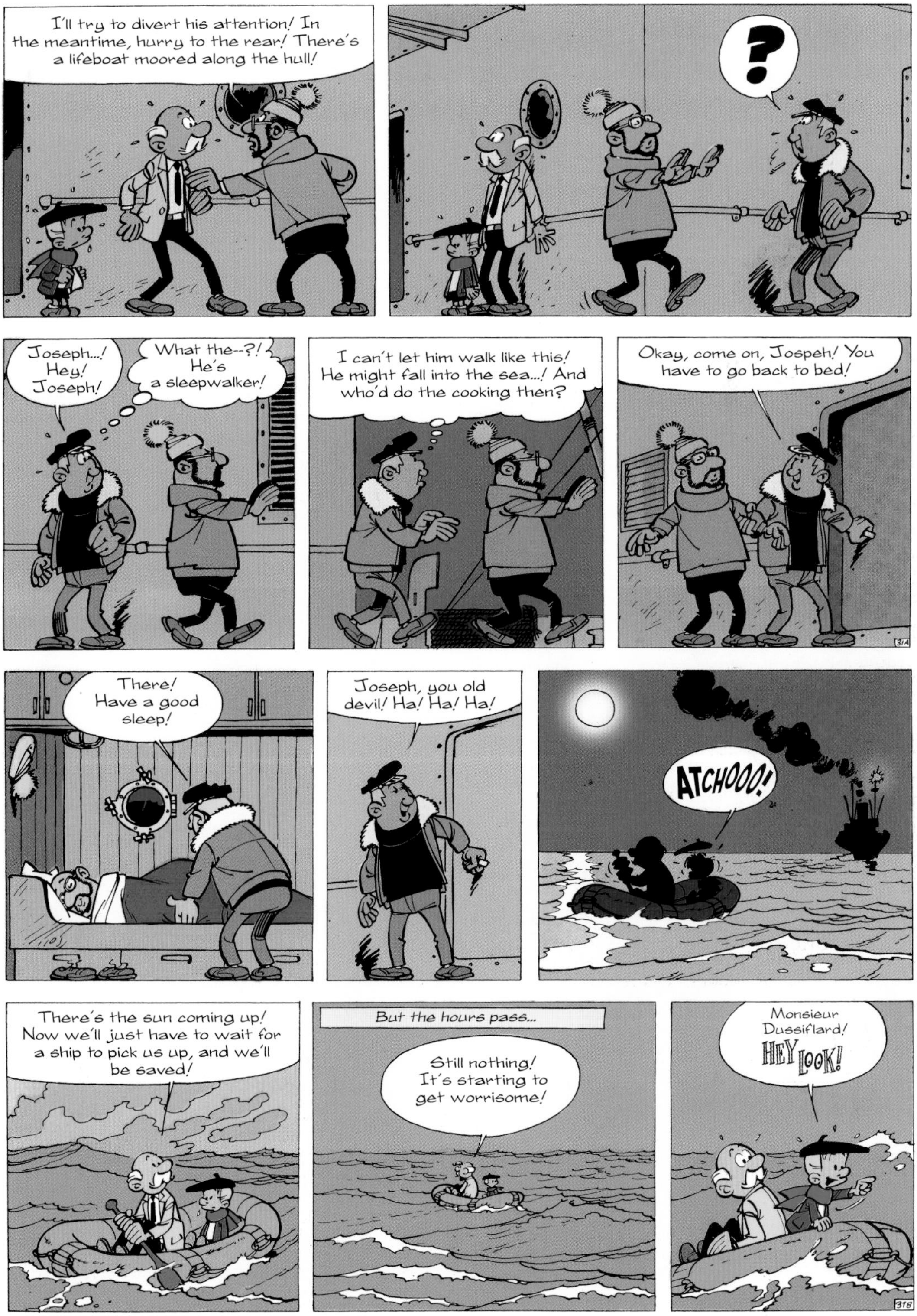

I'll try to divert his attention! In the meantime, hurry to the rear! There's a lifeboat moored along the hull!
?
Joseph...! Hey! Joseph!
What the--?! He's a sleepwalker!
I can't let him walk like this! He might fall into the sea...! And who'd do the cooking then?
Okay, come on, Jospeh! You have to go back to bed!
31A
There! Have a good sleep!
Joseph, you old devil! Ha! Ha! Ha!
ATCHOOO!
There's the sun coming up! Now we'll just have to wait for a ship to pick us up, and we'll be saved!
But the hours pass...
Still nothing! It's starting to get worrisome!
Monsieur Dussiflard! HEY LOOK!
31B

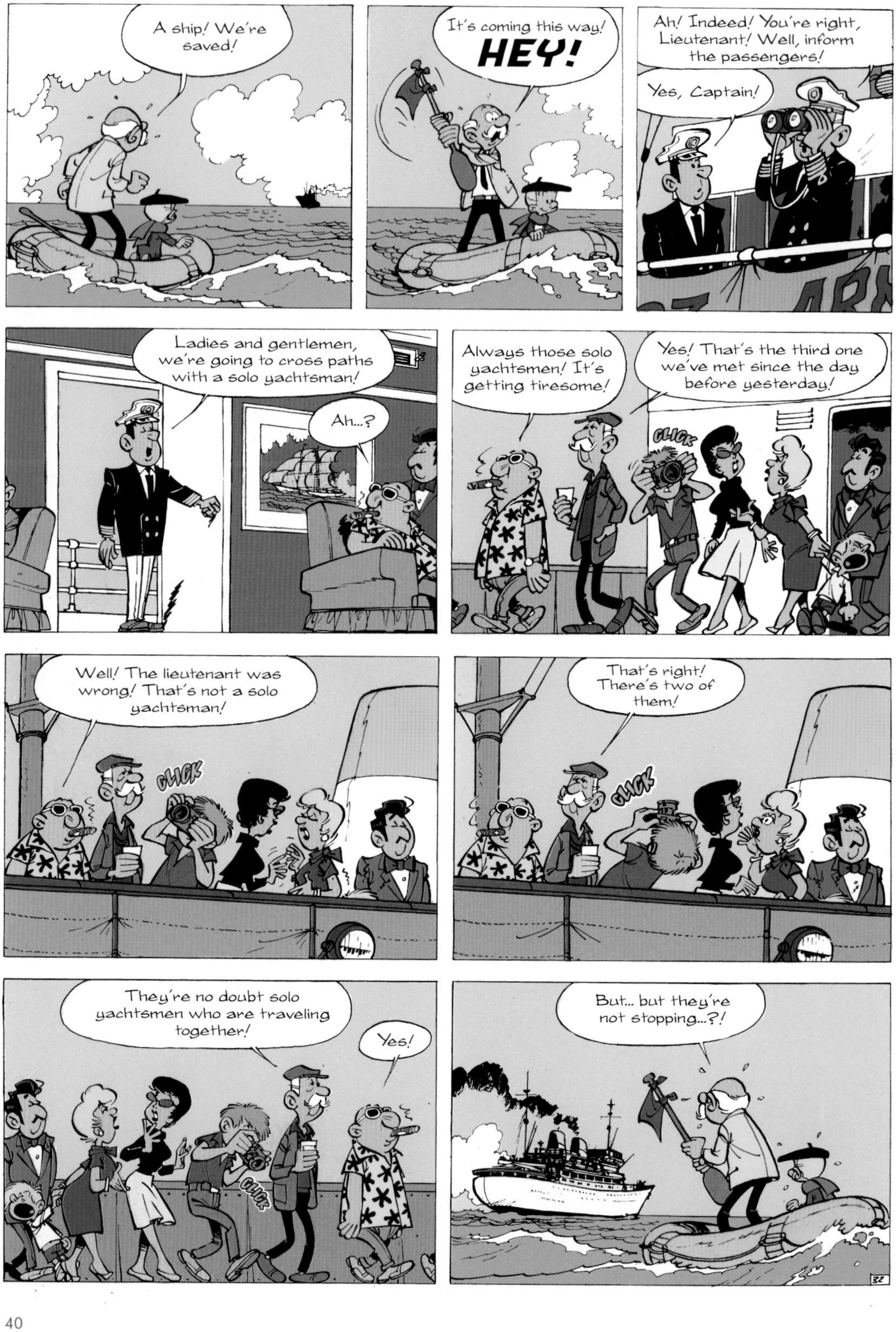
A ship! We're saved!
It's coming this way!
HEY!
Ah! Indeed! You're right, Lieutenant! Well, inform the passengers!
Yes, Captain!
Ladies and gentlemen, we're going to cross paths with a solo yachtsman!
Ah...?
Always those solo yachtsmen! It's getting tiresome!
Yes! That's the third one we've met since the day before yesterday!
CLICK
Well! The lieutenant was wrong! That's not a solo yachtsman!
CLICK
That's right! There's two of them!
CLICK
They're no doubt solo yachtsmen who are traveling together!
Yes!
CLICK
But... but they're not stopping...?!
32

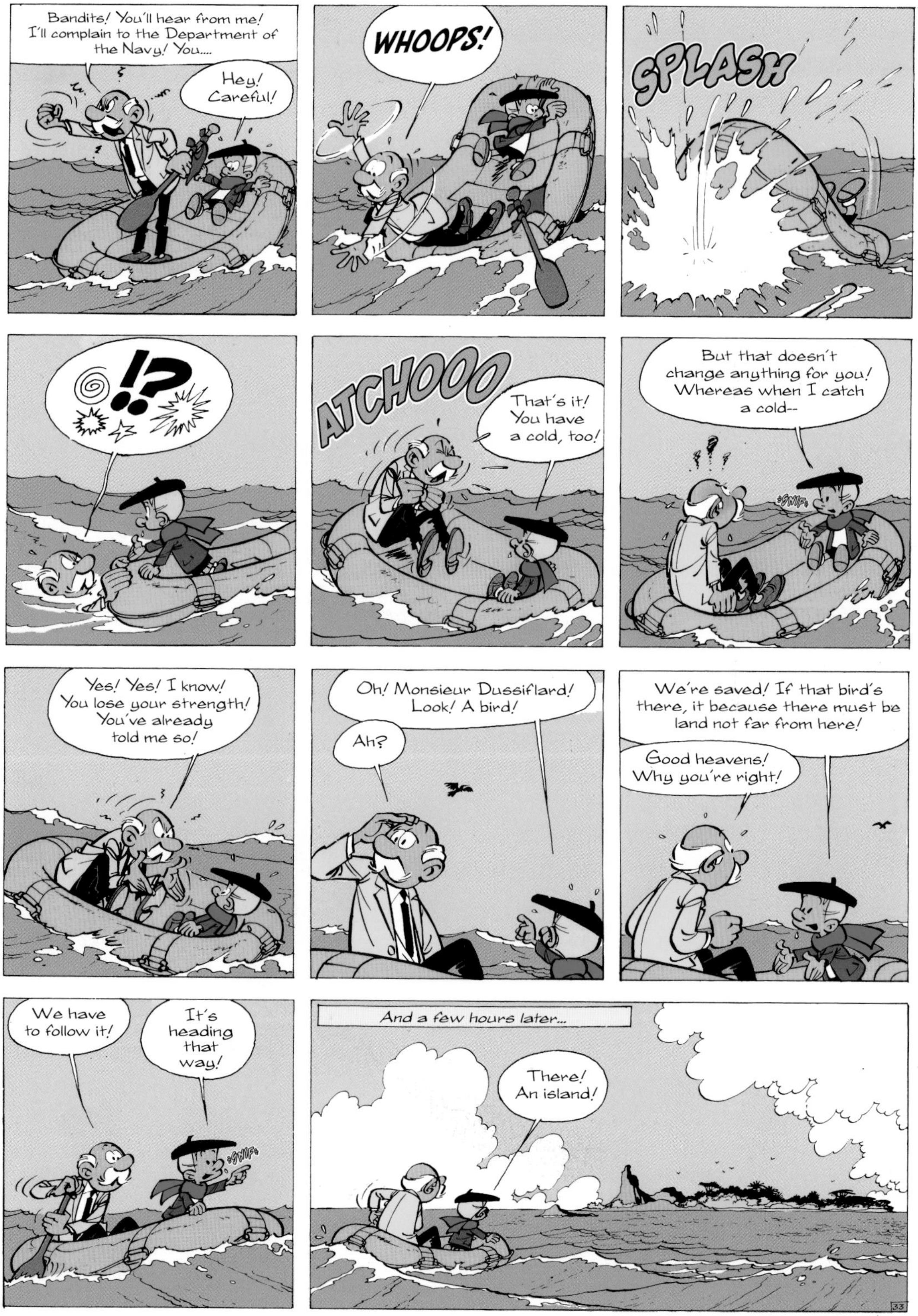
Bandits! You'll hear from me! I'll complain to the Department of the Navy! You....
Hey! Careful!
WHOOPS!
SPLASH
!?
ATCHOOO
That's it! You have a cold, too!
But that doesn't change anything for you! Whereas when I catch a cold--
SNIF
Yes! Yes! I know! You lose your strength! You've already told me so!
Oh! Monsieur Dussiflard! Look! A bird!
Ah?
We're saved! If that bird's there, it because there must be land not far from here!
Good heavens! Why you're right!
We have to follow it!
It's heading that way!
SNIF
And a few hours later...
There! An island!
33

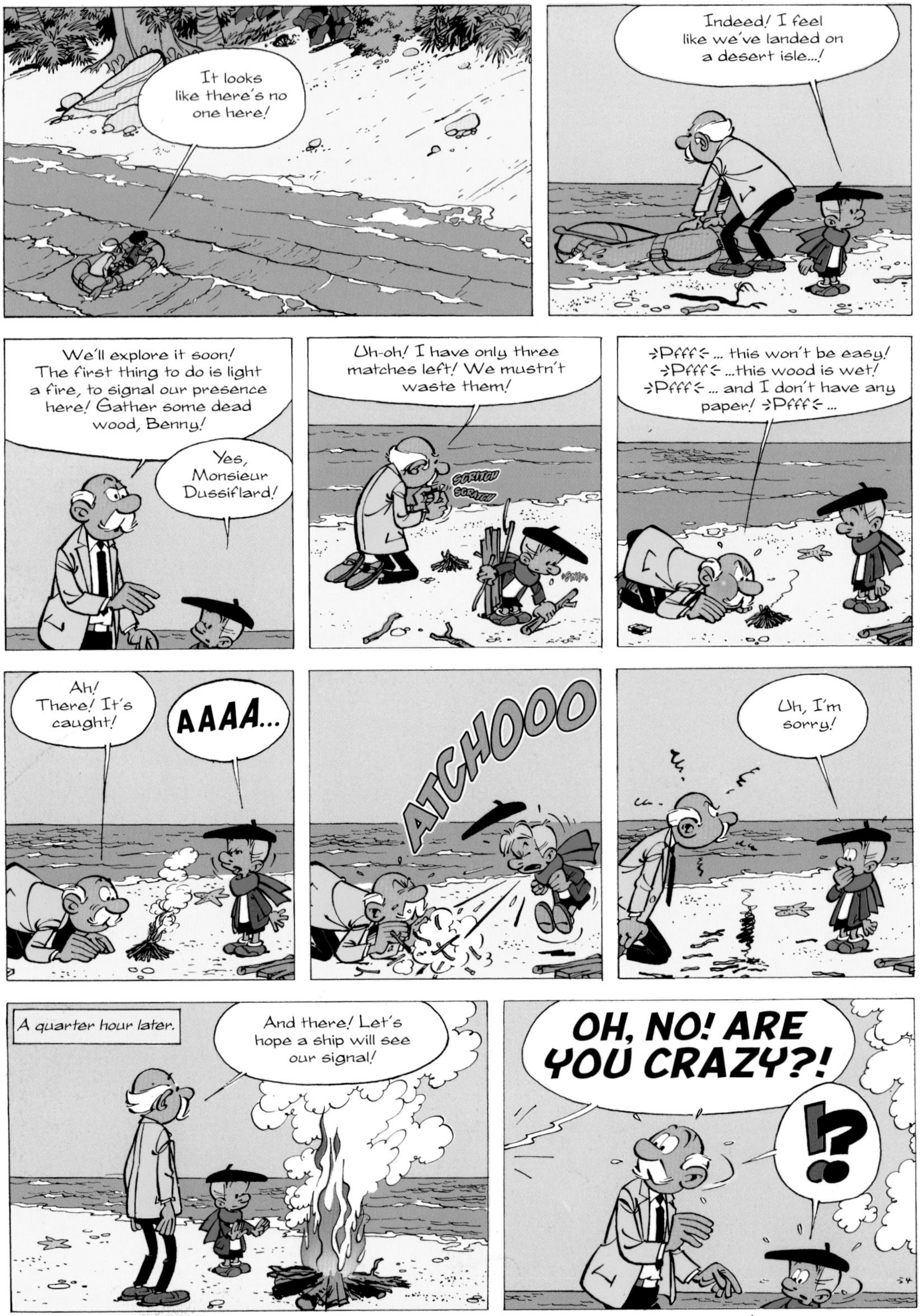

It looks like there's no one here!
Indeed! I feel like we've landed on a desert isle...!
We'll explore it soon! The first thing to do is light a fire, to signal our presence here! Gather some dead wood, Benny!
Yes, Monsieur Dussiflard!
Uh-oh! I have only three matches left! We mustn't waste them!
SCRITCH
SCRATCH
SNIF
>Pfff< ... this won't be easy! >Pfff< ...this wood is wet! >Pfff< ... and I don't have any paper! >Pfff< ...
Ah! There! It's caught!
AAAA...
ATCHOOO
Uh, I'm sorry!
A quarter hour later.
And there! Let's hope a ship will see our signal!
OH, NO! ARE YOU CRAZY?!
!?

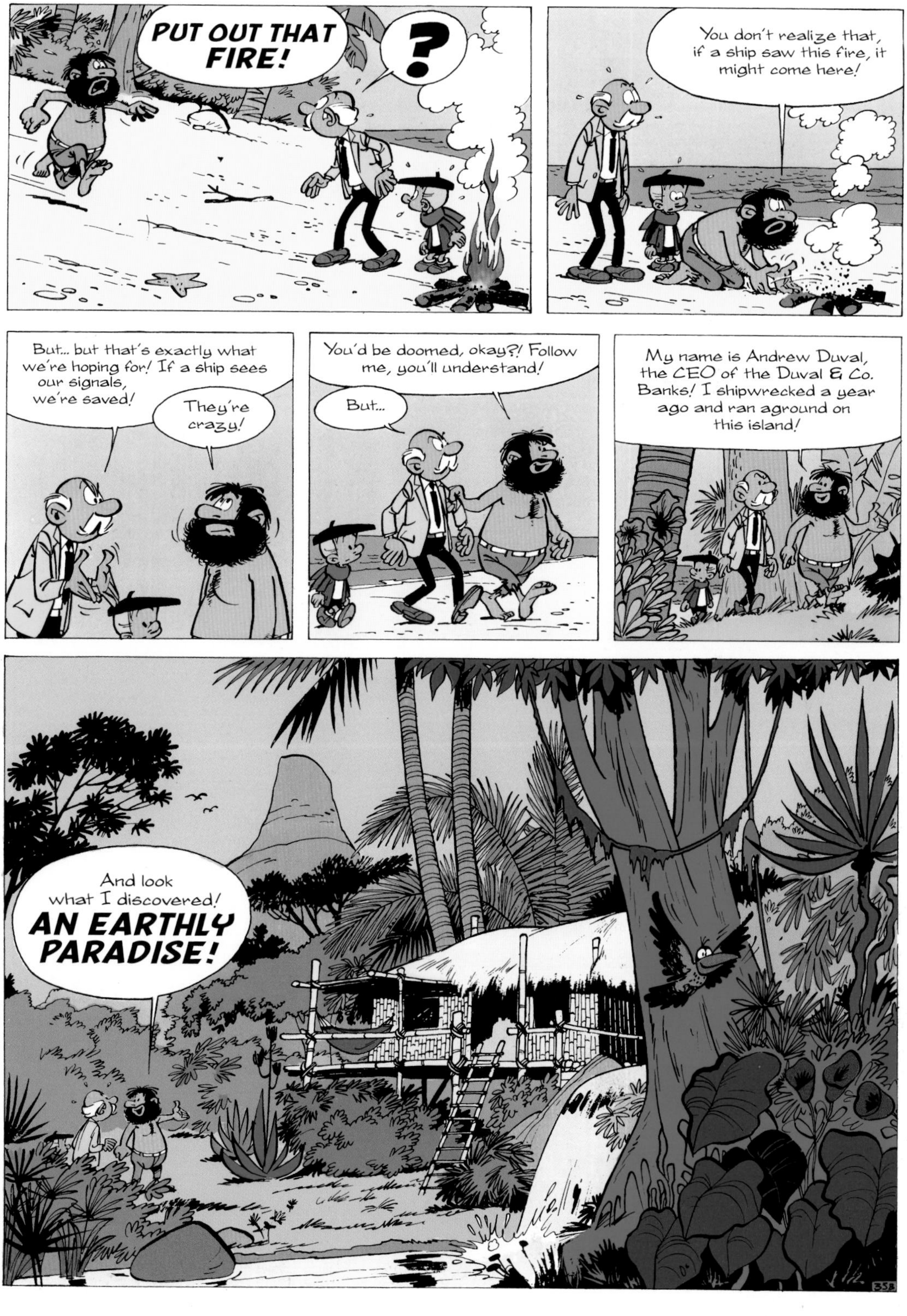
PUT OUT THAT FIRE!
?
You don't realize that, if a ship saw this fire, it might come here!
But... but that's exactly what we're hoping for! If a ship sees our signals, we're saved!
They're crazy!
You'd be doomed, okay?! Follow me, you'll understand!
But...
My name is Andrew Duval, the CEO of the Duval & Co. Banks! I shipwrecked a year ago and ran aground on this island!
And look what I discovered! AN EARTHLY PARADISE!

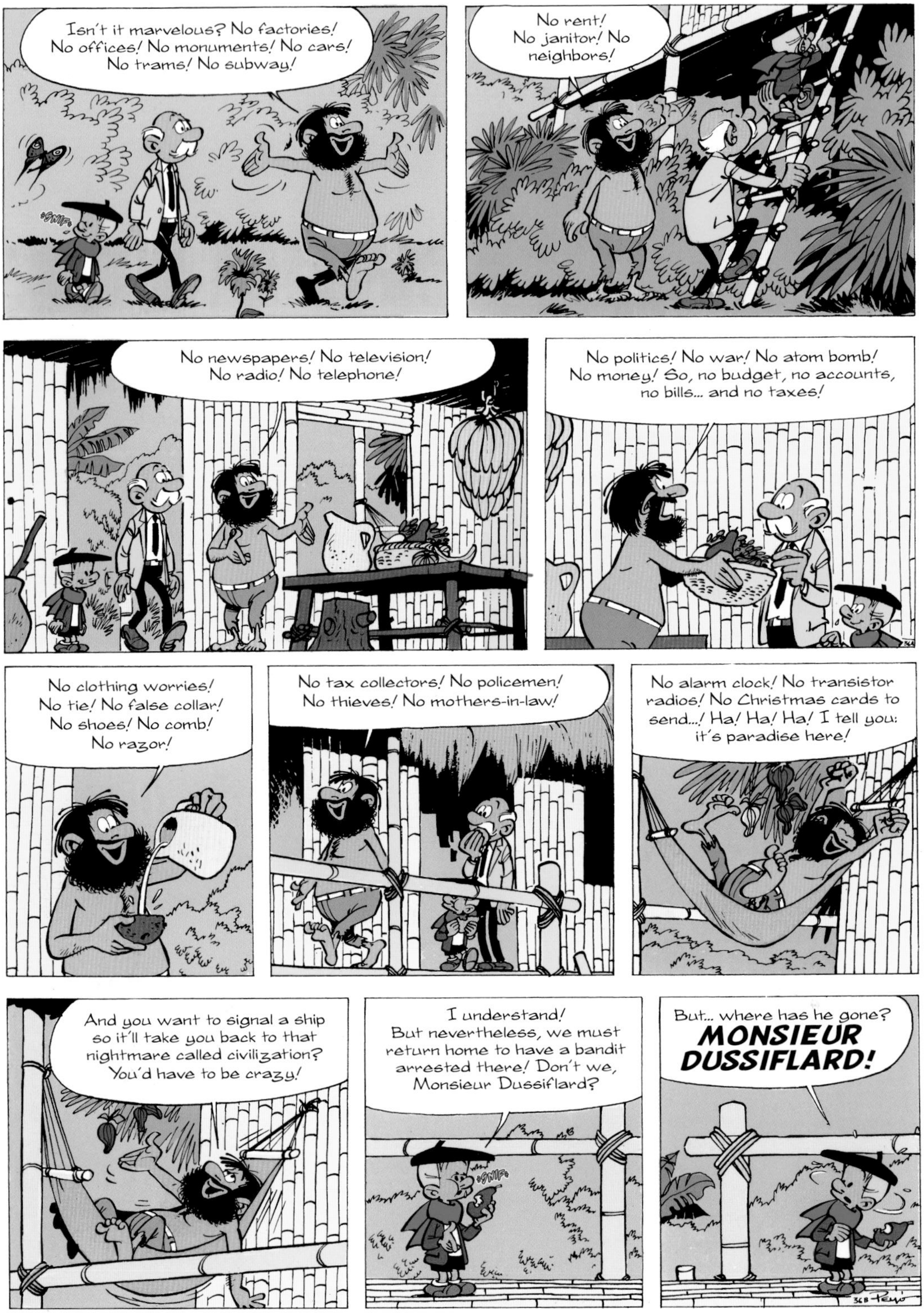
Isn't it marvelous? No factories! No offices! No monuments! No cars! No trams! No subway!
SNIF
No rent! No janitor! No neighbors!
No newspapers! No television! No radio! No telephone!
No politics! No war! No atom bomb! No money! So, no budget, no accounts, no bills... and no taxes!
No clothing worries! No tie! No false collar! No shoes! No comb! No razor!
No tax collectors! No policemen! No thieves! No mothers-in-law!
No alarm clock! No transistor radios! No Christmas cards to send...! Ha! Ha! Ha! I tell you: it's paradise here!
And you want to signal a ship so it'll take you back to that nightmare called civilization? You'd have to be crazy!
I understand! But nevertheless, we must return home to have a bandit arrested there! Don't we, Monsieur Dussiflard?
SNIF
But... where has he gone? MONSIEUR DUSSIFLARD!

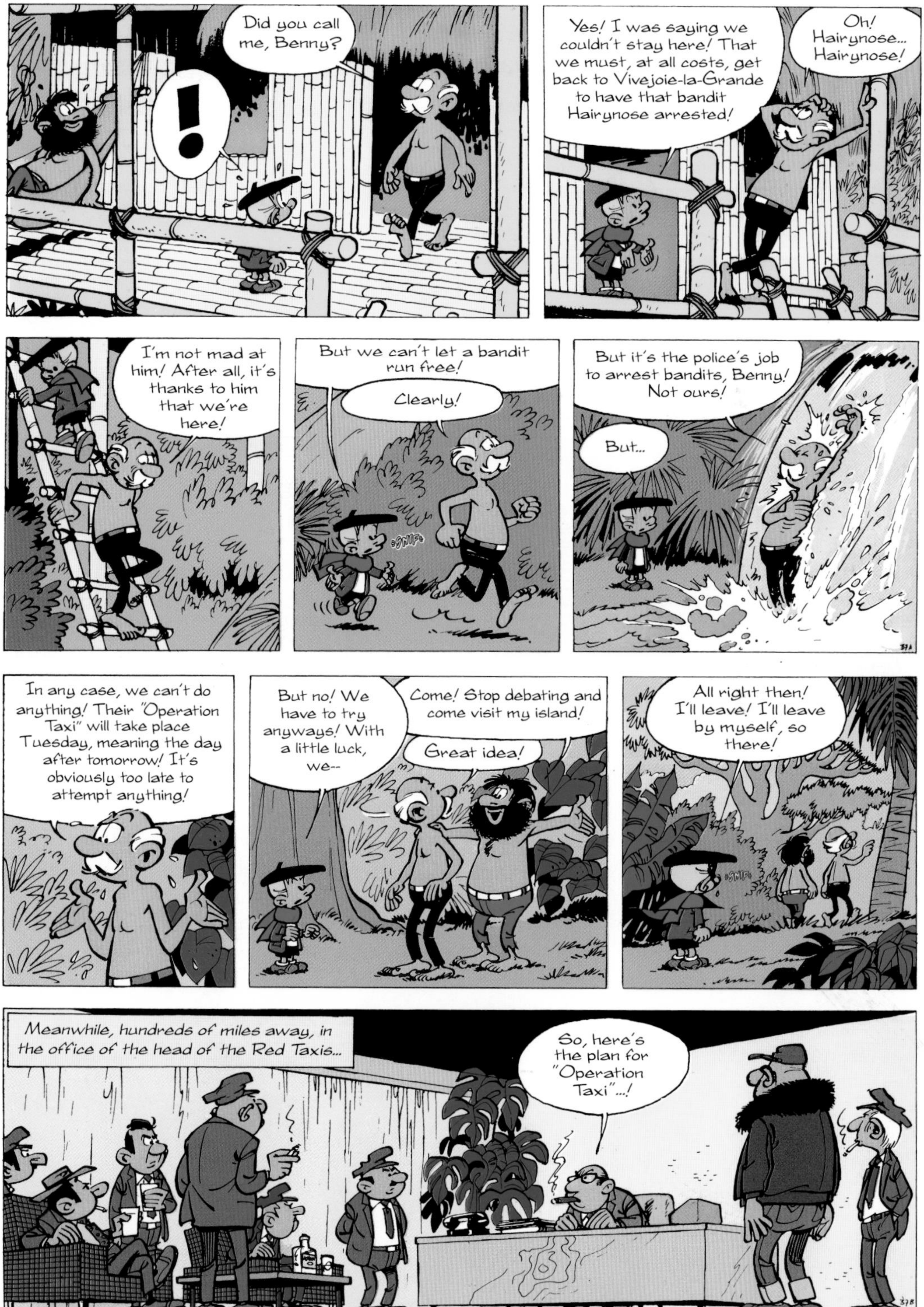
!
Did you call me, Benny?
Yes! I was saying we couldn't stay here! That we must, at all costs, get back to Vivejoie-la-Grande to have that bandit Hairynose arrested!
Oh! Hairynose... Hairynose!
I'm not mad at him! After all, it's thanks to him that we're here!
But we can't let a bandit run free!
Clearly!
SNIF
But it's the police's job to arrest bandits, Benny! Not ours!
But...
In any case, we can't do anything! Their "Operation Taxi" will take place Tuesday, meaning the day after tomorrow! It's obviously too late to attempt anything!
But no! We have to try anyways! With a little luck, we--
Come! Stop debating and come visit my island!
Great idea!
All right then! I'll leave! I'll leave by myself, so there!
SNIF
Meanwhile, hundreds of miles away, in the office of the head of the Red Taxis...
So, here's the plan for "Operation Taxi"...!

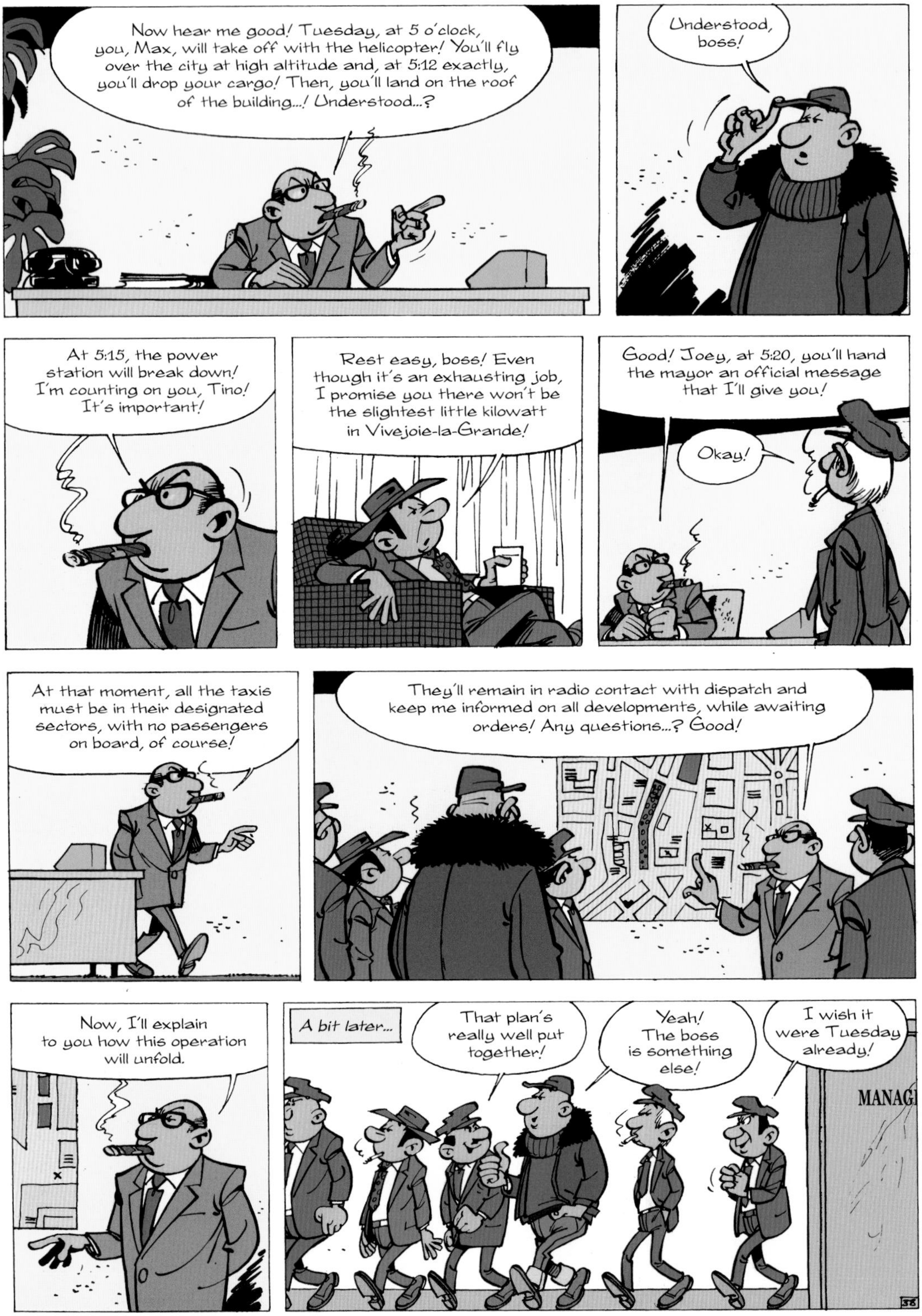

Now hear me good! Tuesday, at 5 o'clock, you, Max, will take off with the helicopter! You'll fly over the city at high altitude and, at 5:12 exactly, you'll drop your cargo! Then, you'll land on the roof of the building...! Understood...?
Understood, boss!
At 5:15, the power station will break down! I'm counting on you, Tino! It's important!
Rest easy, boss! Even though it's an exhausting job, I promise you there won't be the slightest little kilowatt in Vivejoie-la-Grande!
Good! Joey, at 5:20, you'll hand the mayor an official message that I'll give you!
Okay!
At that moment, all the taxis must be in their designated sectors, with no passengers on board, of course!
They'll remain in radio contact with dispatch and keep me informed on all developments, while awaiting orders! Any questions...? Good!
Now, I'll explain to you how this operation will unfold.
A bit later...
That plan's really well put together!
Yeah! The boss is something else!
I wish it were Tuesday already!
MANAG

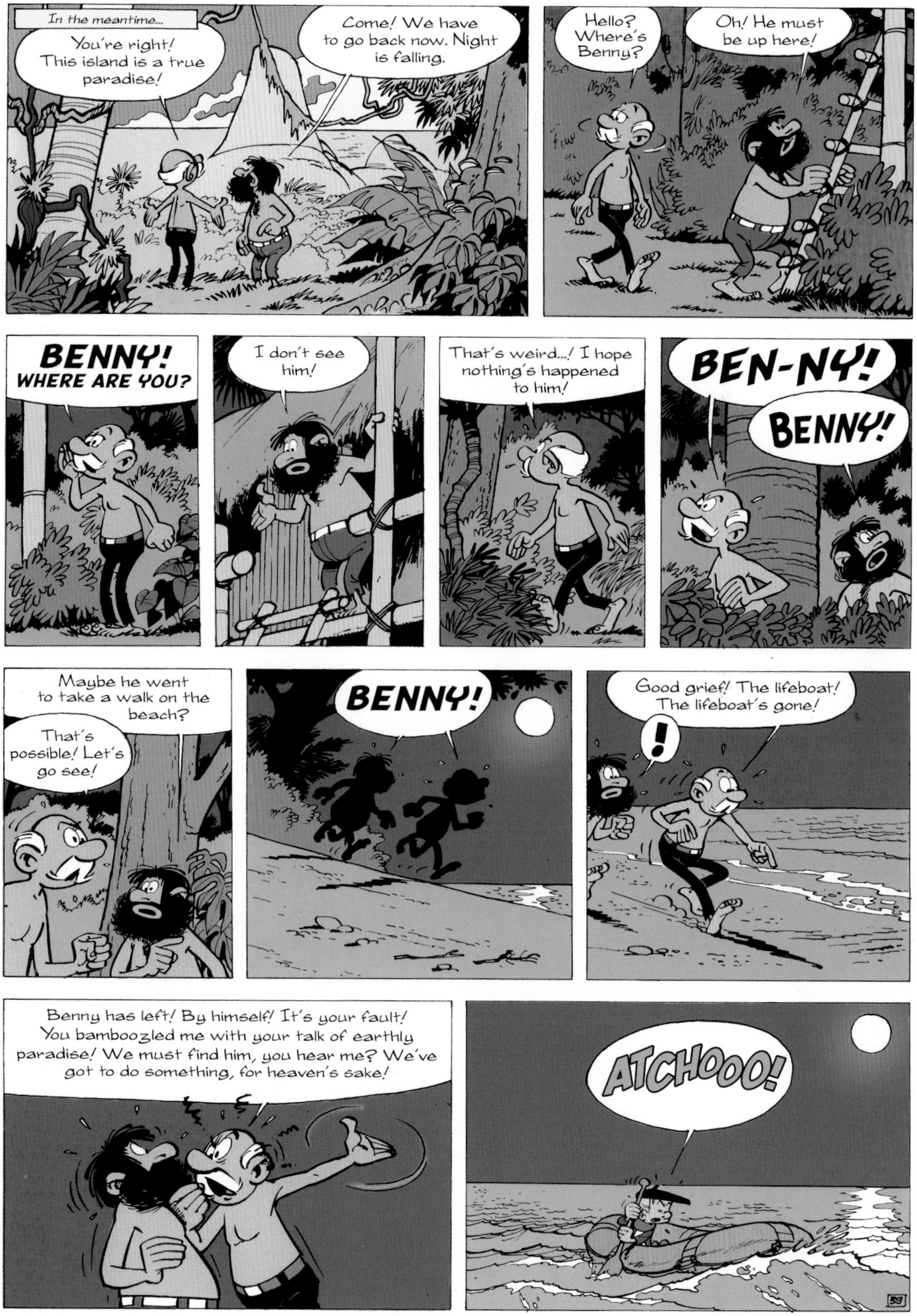
In the meantime...
You're right! This island is a true paradise!
Come! We have to go back now. Night is falling.
Hello? Where's Benny?
Oh! He must be up here!
BENNY! WHERE ARE YOU?
I don't see him!
That's weird...! I hope nothing's happened to him!
BEN-NY!
BENNY!
Maybe he went to take a walk on the beach?
That's possible! Let's go see!
BENNY!
Good grief! The lifeboat! The lifeboat's gone!
!
Benny has left! By himself! It's your fault! You bamboozled me with your talk of earthly paradise! We must find him, you hear me? We've got to do something, for heaven's sake!
ATCHOOO!

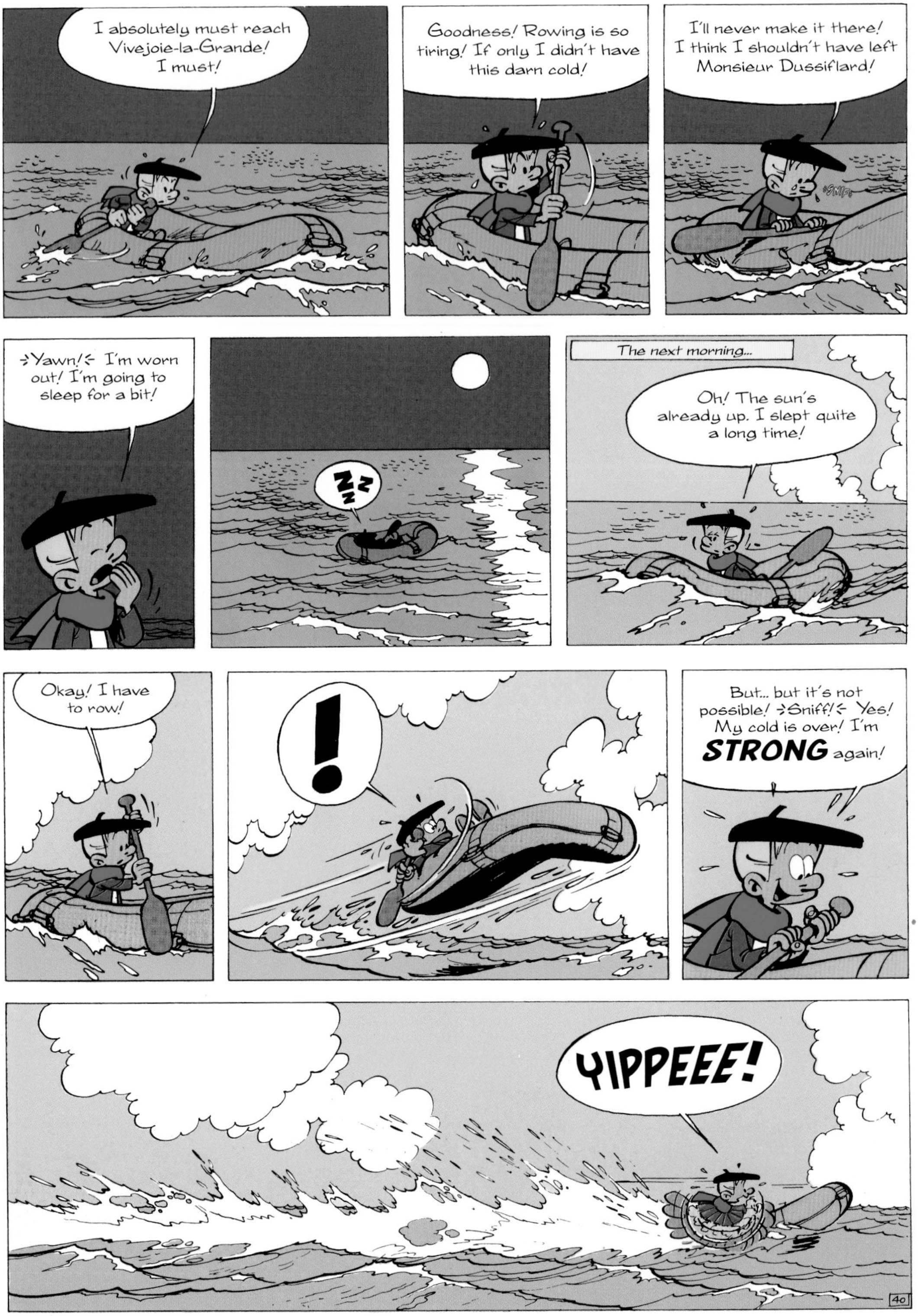
I absolutely must reach Vivejoie-la-Grande! I must!
Goodness! Rowing is so tiring! If only I didn't have this darn cold!
I'll never make it there! I think I shouldn't have left Monsieur Dussiflard!
SNIF
→Yawn!← I'm worn out! I'm going to sleep for a bit!
ZZZ
The next morning...
Oh! The sun's already up. I slept quite a long time!
Okay! I have to row!
!
But... but it's not possible! →Sniff!← Yes! My cold is over! I'm STRONG again!
YIPPEEE!
40

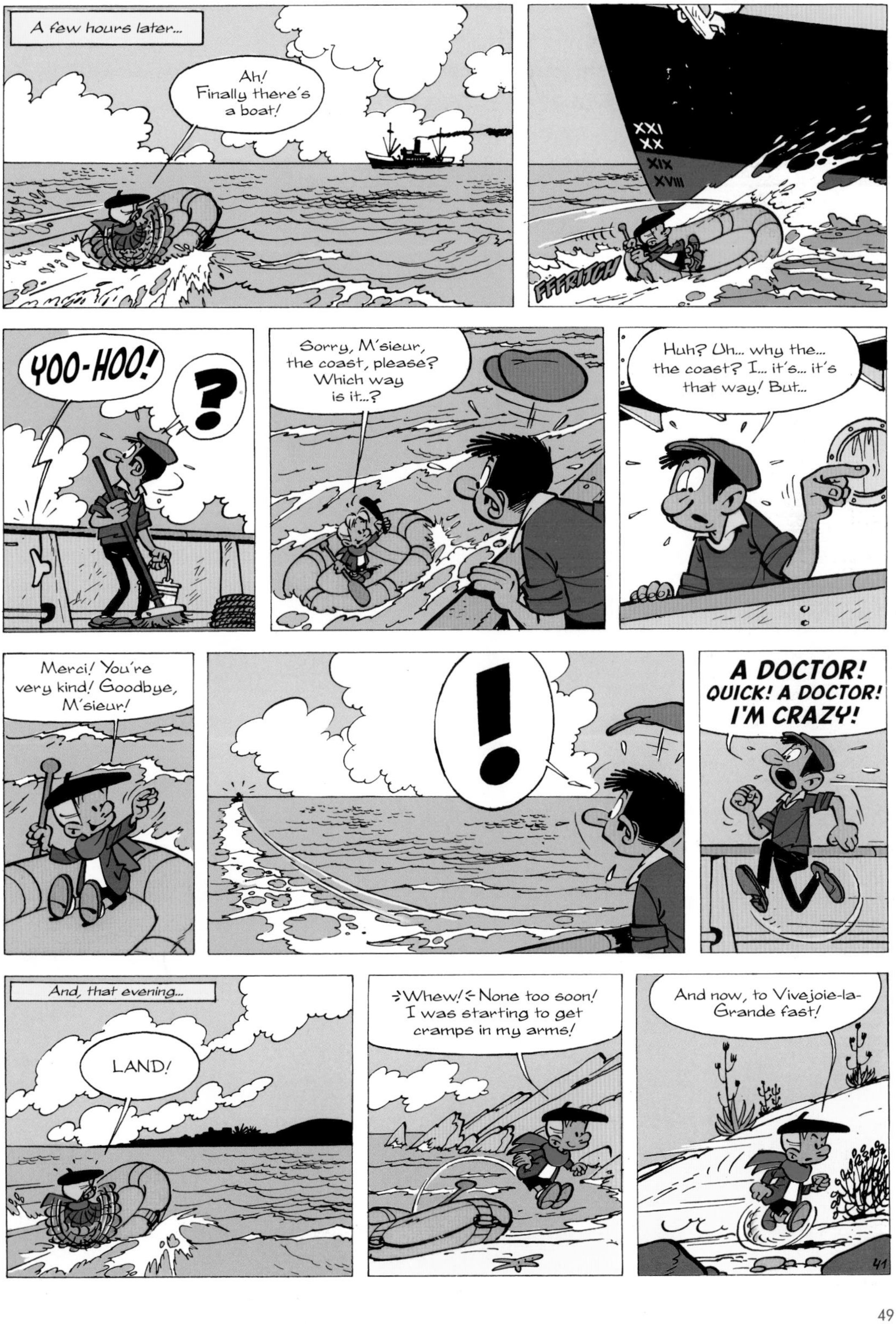
A few hours later...
Ah! Finally there's a boat!
XXI
XX
XIX
XVIII
FFFRITCH
YOO-HOO!
?
Sorry, M'sieur, the coast, please? Which way is it...?
Huh? Uh... why the... the coast? I... it's... it's that way! But...
Merci! You're very kind! Goodbye, M'sieur!
!
A DOCTOR! QUICK! A DOCTOR! I'M CRAZY!
And, that evening...
LAND!
Whew! None too soon! I was starting to get cramps in my arms!
And now, to Vivejoie-la-Grande fast!
41

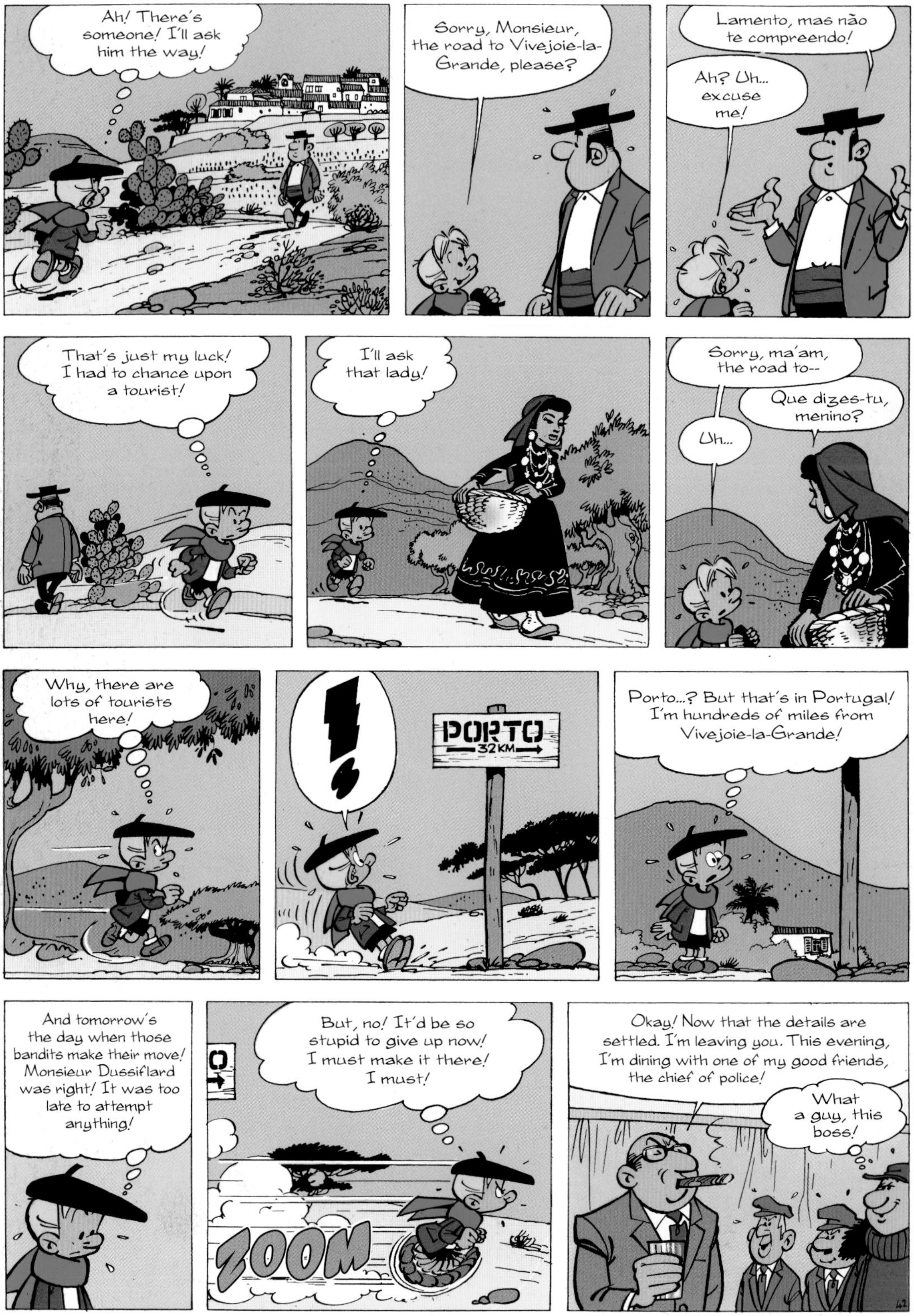
Ah! There's someone! I'll ask him the way!
Sorry, Monsieur, the road to Vivejoie-la-Grande, please?
Lamento, mas não te compreendo!
Ah? Uh... excuse me!
That's just my luck! I had to chance upon a tourist!
I'll ask that lady!
Sorry, ma'am, the road to--
Que dizes-tu, menino?
Uh...
Why, there are lots of tourists here!
PORTO
32 KM
Porto...? But that's in Portugal! I'm hundreds of miles from Vivejoie-la-Grande!
And tomorrow's the day when those bandits make their move! Monsieur Dussiflard was right! It was too late to attempt anything!
But, no! It'd be so stupid to give up now! I must make it there! I must!
ZOOM
Okay! Now that the details are settled, I'm leaving you. This evening, I'm dining with one of my good friends, the chief of police!
What a guy, this boss!

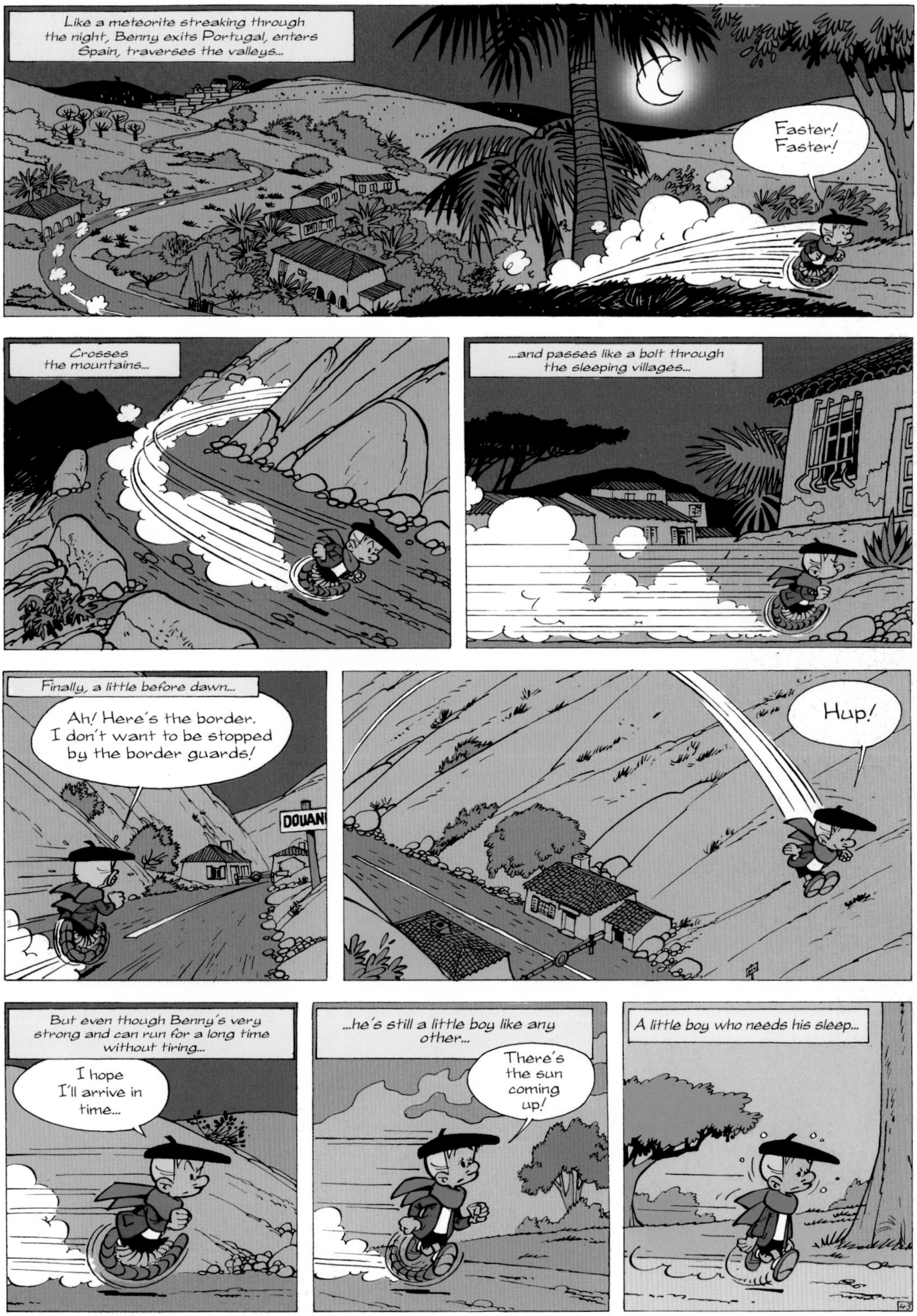

Like a meteorite streaking through the night, Benny exits Portugal, enters Spain, traverses the valleys...
Faster! Faster!
Crosses the mountains...
...and passes like a bolt through the sleeping villages...
Finally, a little before dawn...
Ah! Here's the border. I don't want to be stopped by the border guards!
DOUAN
Hup!
But even though Benny's very strong and can run for a long time without tiring...
I hope I'll arrive in time...
...he's still a little boy like any other...
There's the sun coming up!
A little boy who needs his sleep...

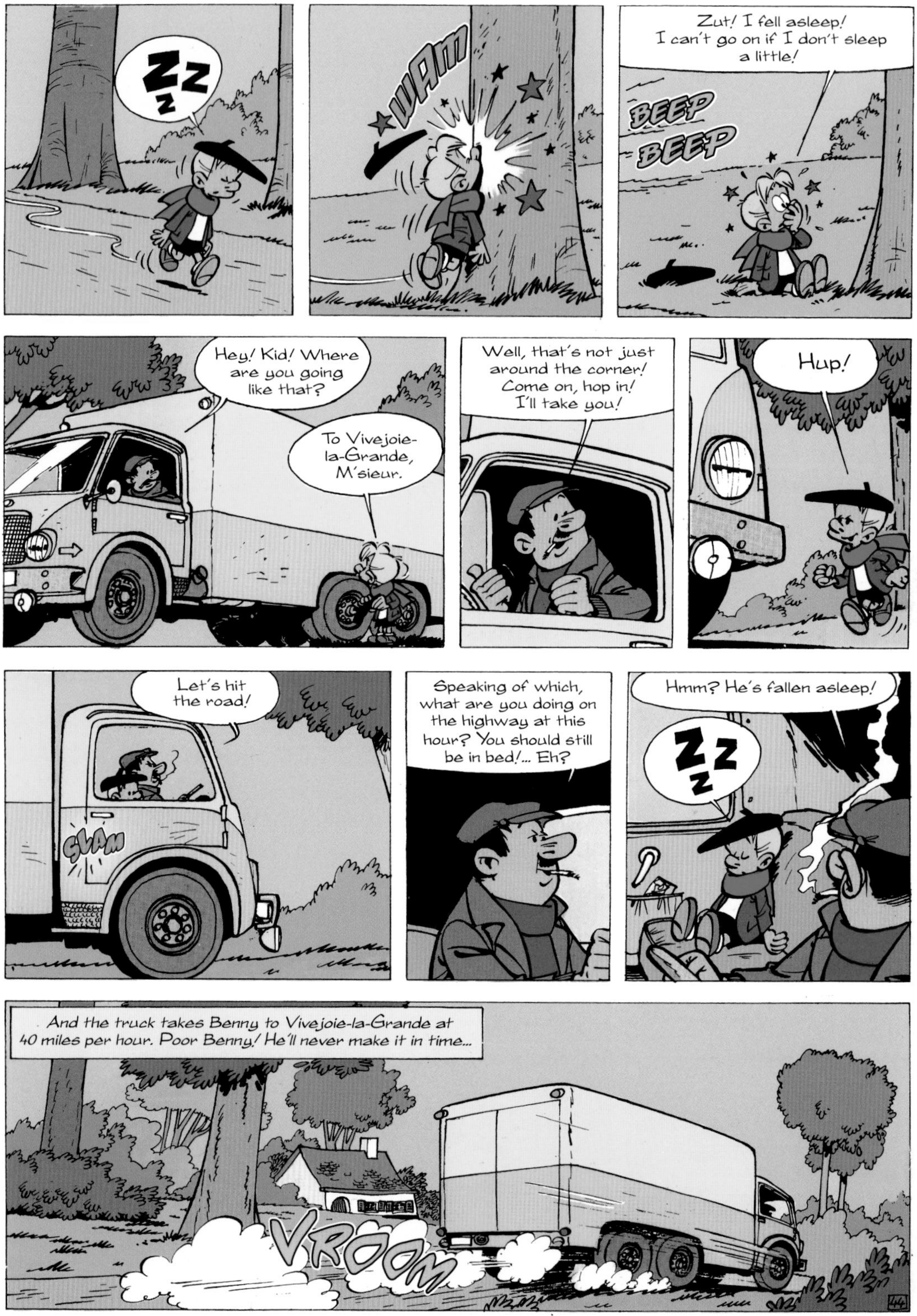
ZZZ
WAM
Zut! I fell asleep! I can't go on if I don't sleep a little!
BEEP BEEP
Hey! Kid! Where are you going like that?
To Vivejoie-la-Grande, M'sieur.
Well, that's not just around the corner! Come on, hop in! I'll take you!
Hup!
Let's hit the road!
SLAM
Speaking of which, what are you doing on the highway at this hour? You should still be in bed!... Eh?
Hmm? He's fallen asleep!
ZZZ
And the truck takes Benny to Vivejoie-la-Grande at 40 miles per hour. Poor Benny! He'll never make it in time...
VROOM
44

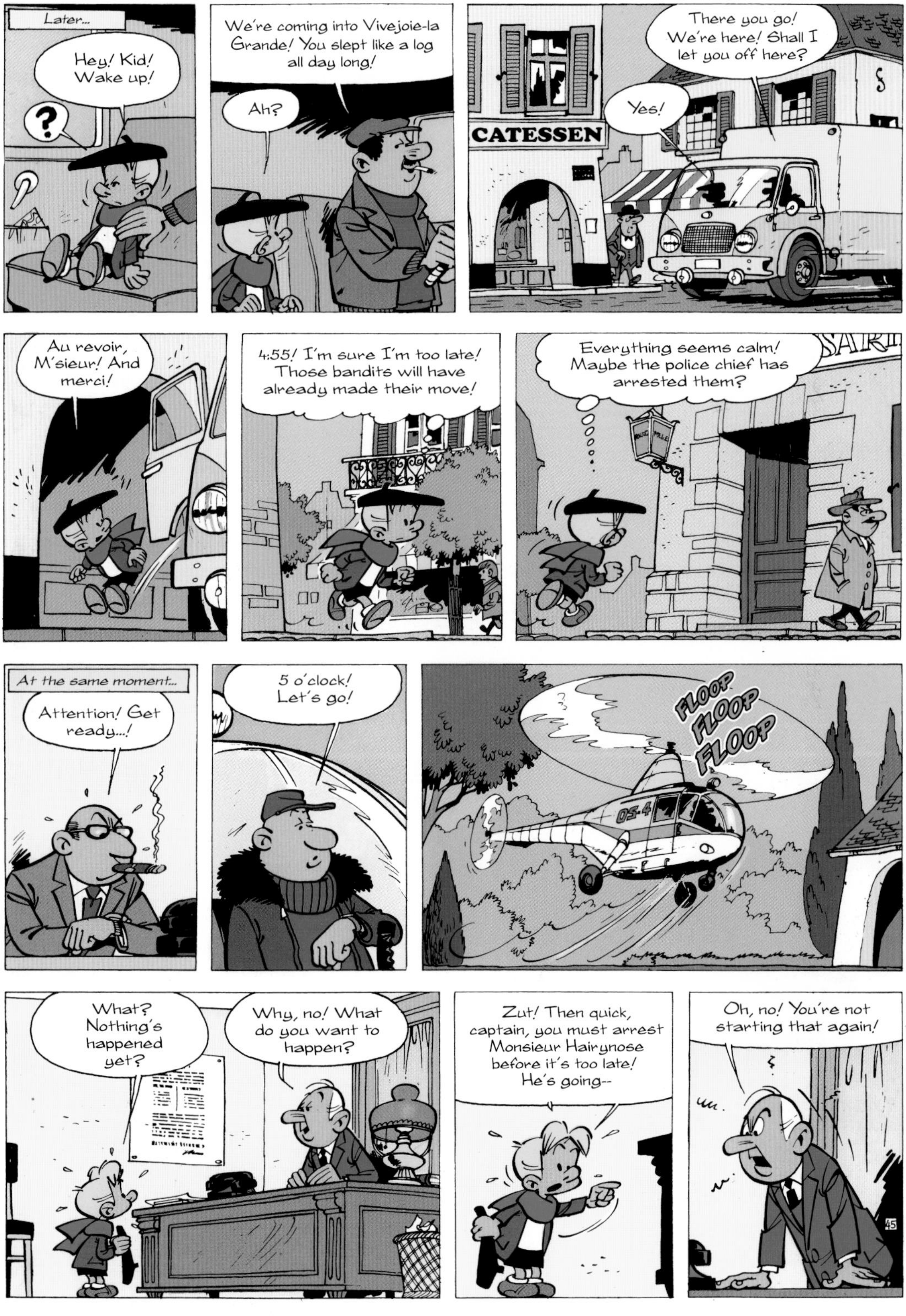
Later...
Hey! Kid! Wake up!
?
We're coming into Vivejoie-la Grande! You slept like a log all day long!
Ah?
There you go! We're here! Shall I let you off here?
Yes!
CATESSEN
Au revoir, M'sieur! And merci!
4:55! I'm sure I'm too late! Those bandits will have already made their move!
Everything seems calm! Maybe the police chief has arrested them?
At the same moment...
Attention! Get ready...!
5 o'clock! Let's go!
FLOOP FLOOP FLOOP
OS-4
What? Nothing's happened yet?
Why, no! What do you want to happen?
Zut! Then quick, captain, you must arrest Monsieur Hairynose before it's too late! He's going--
Oh, no! You're not starting that again!

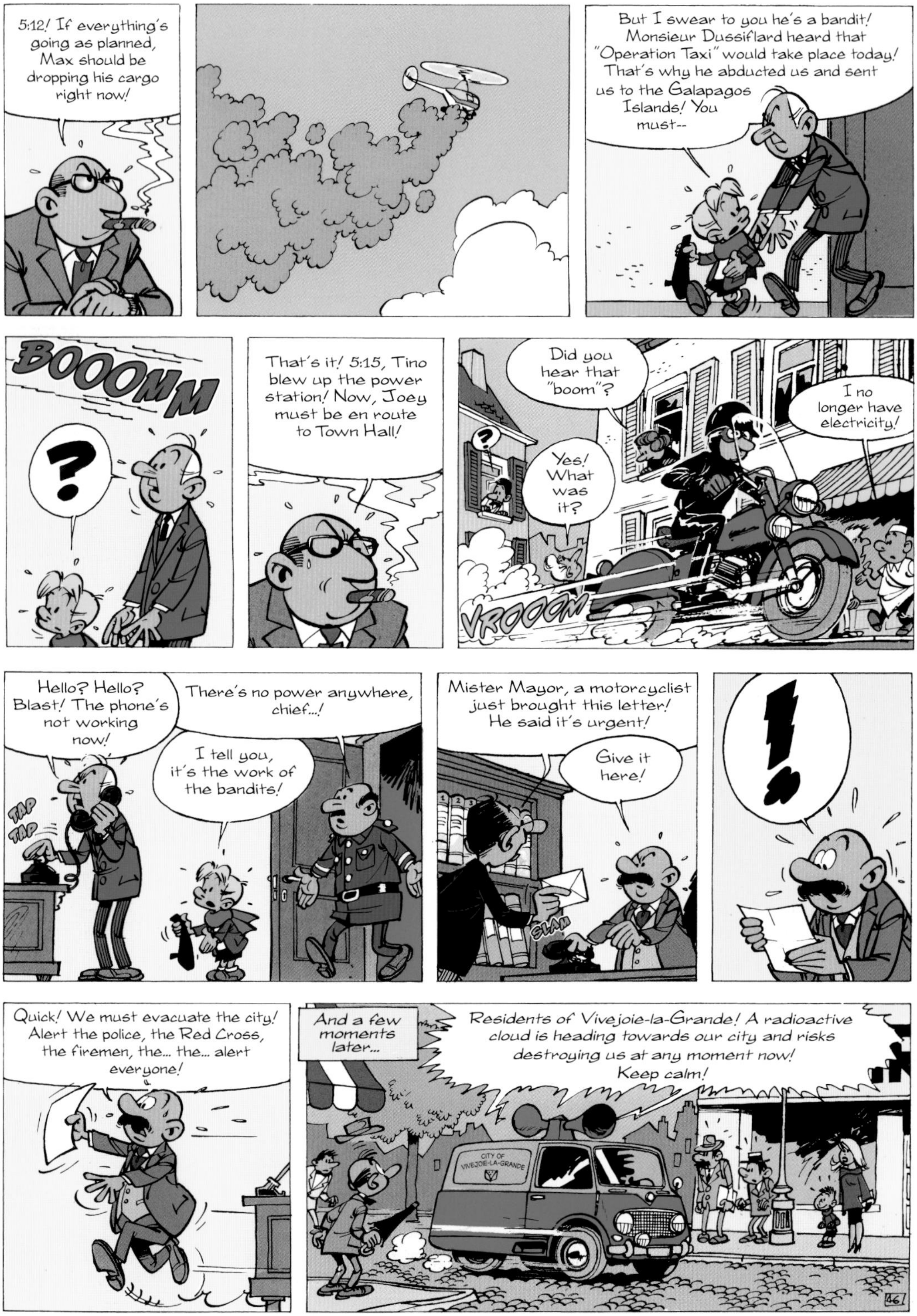

5:12! If everything's going as planned, Max should be dropping his cargo right now!
But I swear to you he's a bandit! Monsieur Dussiflard heard that "Operation Taxi" would take place today! That's why he abducted us and sent us to the Galapagos Islands! You must--
BOOOMM
?
That's it! 5:15, Tino blew up the power station! Now, Joey must be en route to Town Hall!
Did you hear that "boom"?
?
Yes! What was it?
I no longer have electricity!
VROOOM
Hello? Hello? Blast! The phone's not working now!
TAP TAP
There's no power anywhere, chief...!
I tell you, it's the work of the bandits!
Mister Mayor, a motorcyclist just brought this letter! He said it's urgent!
Give it here!
SLAM
!
Quick! We must evacuate the city! Alert the police, the Red Cross, the firemen, the... the... alert everyone!
And a few moments later...
Residents of Vivejoie-la-Grande! A radioactive cloud is heading towards our city and risks destroying us at any moment now! Keep calm!
CITY OF VIVEJOIE-LA-GRANDE
46

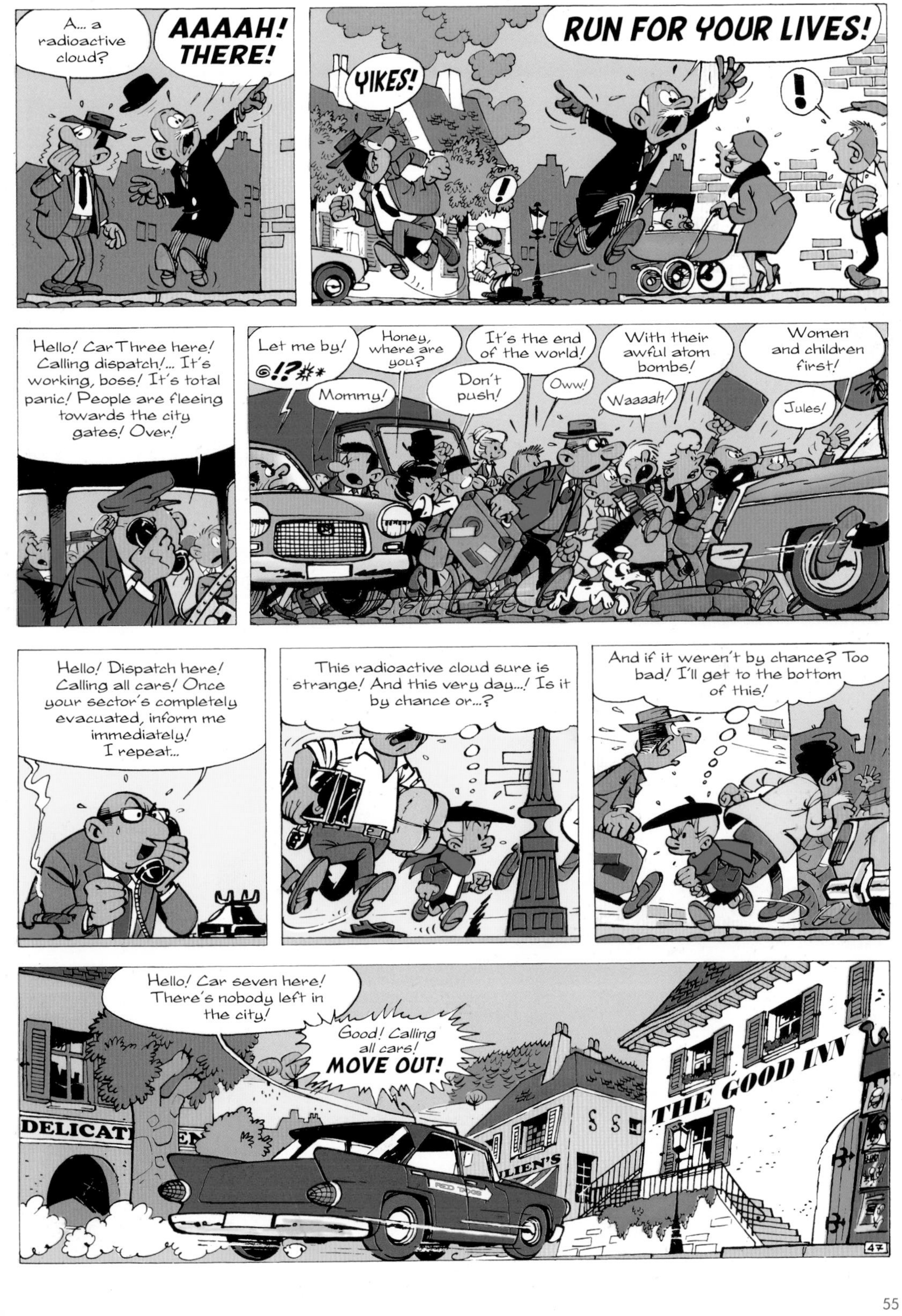
A... a radioactive cloud?
AAAAH! THERE!
RUN FOR YOUR LIVES!
YIKES!
!
!
Hello! Car Three here! Calling dispatch!... It's working, boss! It's total panic! People are fleeing towards the city gates! Over!
Let me by! @!?#*
Honey, where are you?
It's the end of the world!
With their awful atom bombs!
Women and children first!
Mommy!
Don't push!
Oww!
Waaaah!
Jules!
Hello! Dispatch here! Calling all cars! Once your sector's completely evacuated, inform me immediately! I repeat...
This radioactive cloud sure is strange! And this very day...! Is it by chance or...?
And if it weren't by chance? Too bad! I'll get to the bottom of this!
Hello! Car seven here! There's nobody left in the city!
Good! Calling all cars! MOVE OUT!
THE GOOD INN
47

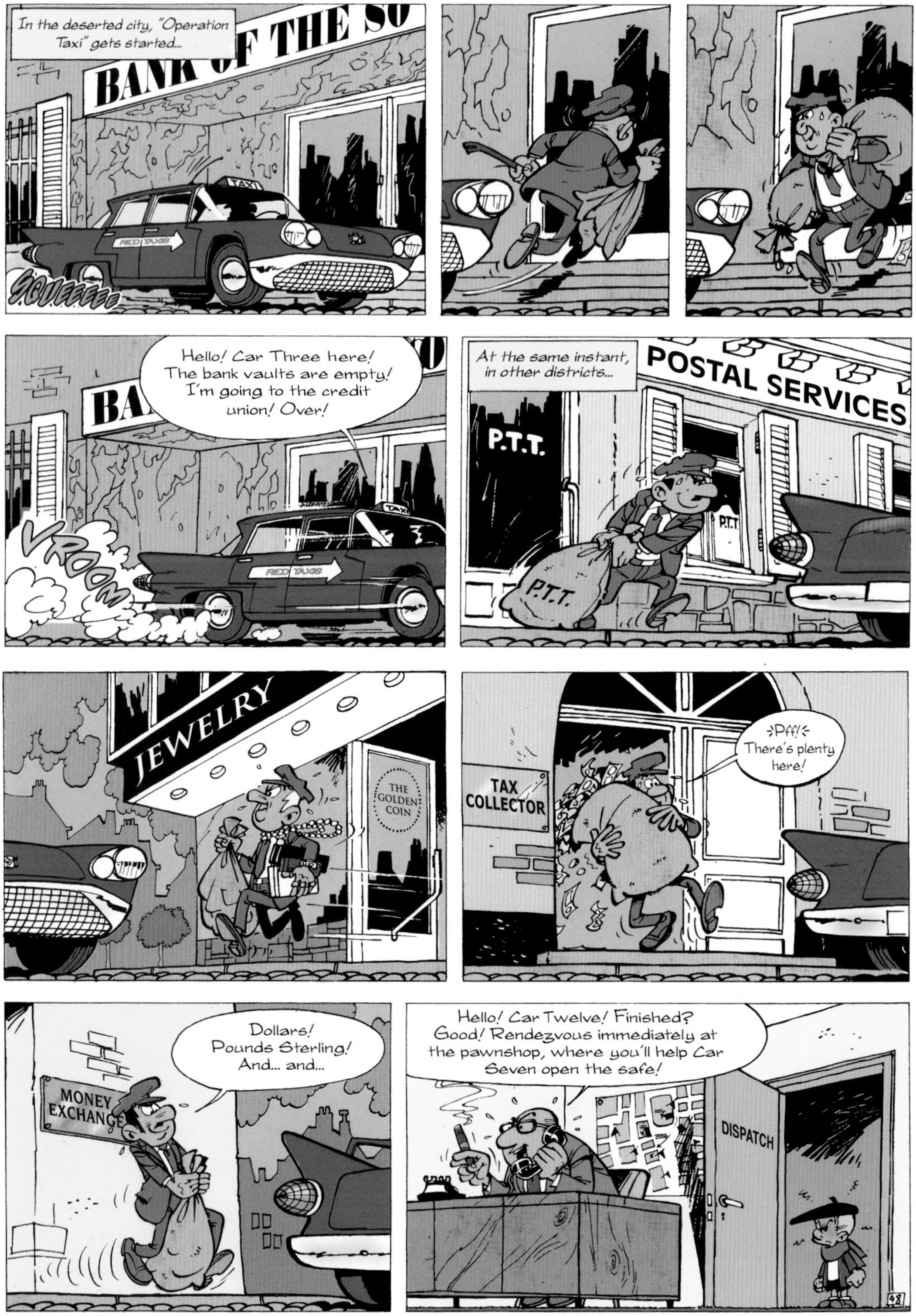

In the deserted city, "Operation Taxi" gets started...
BANK OF THE SO
TAXI
RED TAXIS
SQUEEEEEE
Hello! Car Three here! The bank vaults are empty! I'm going to the credit union! Over!
BA
RED TAXIS
VROOM
At the same instant, in other districts...
POSTAL SERVICES
P.T.T.
P.T.T.
P.T.T.
JEWELRY
THE GOLDEN COIN
TAX COLLECTOR
Pff! There's plenty here!
MONEY EXCHANGE
Dollars! Pounds Sterling! And... and...
Hello! Car Twelve! Finished? Good! Rendezvous immediately at the pawnshop, where you'll help Car Seven open the safe!
DISPATCH
48

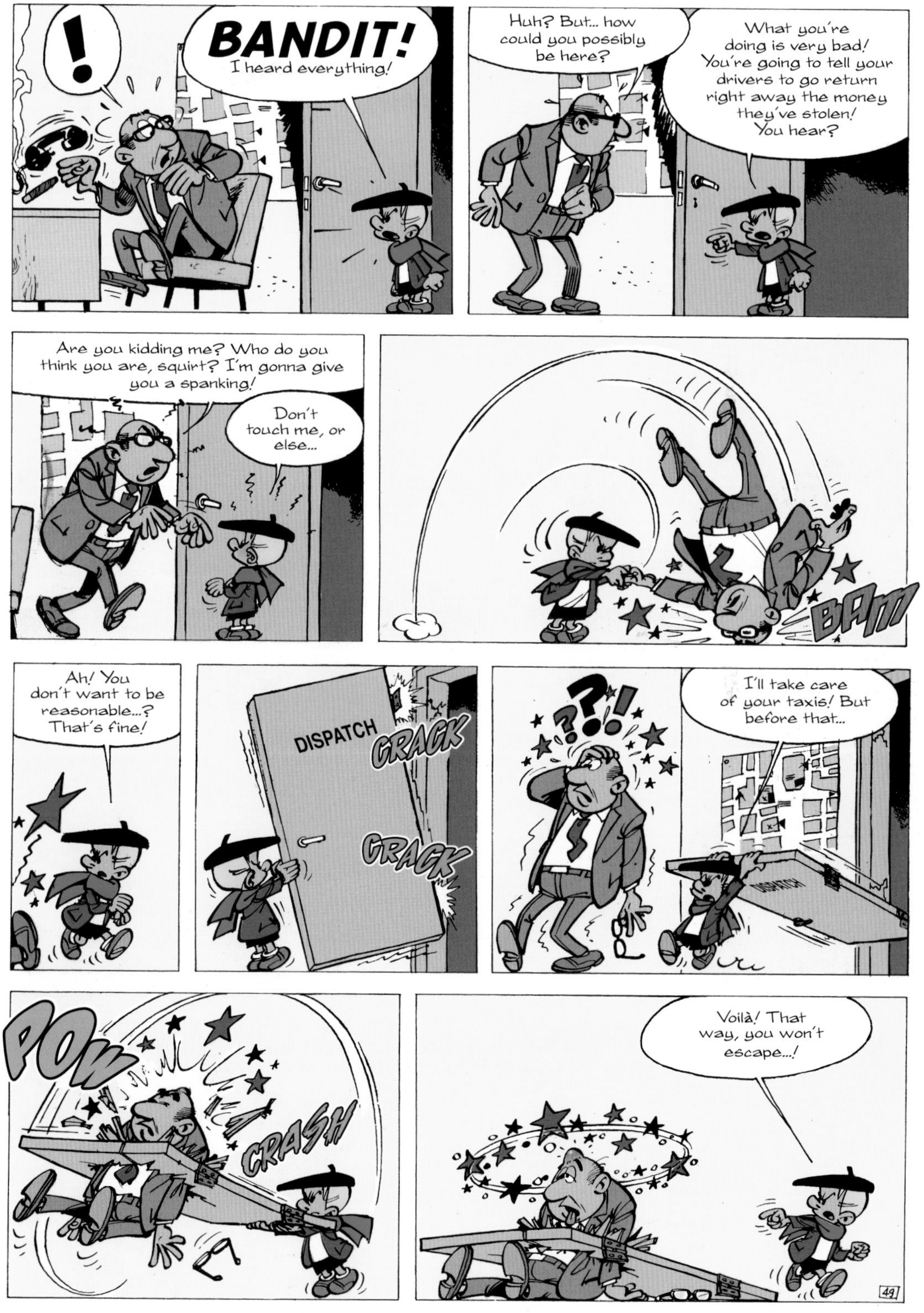
!
BANDIT! I heard everything!
Huh? But... how could you possibly be here?
What you're doing is very bad! You're going to tell your drivers to go return right away the money they've stolen! You hear?
Are you kidding me? Who do you think you are, squirt? I'm gonna give you a spanking!
Don't touch me, or else...
BAM
Ah! You don't want to be reasonable...? That's fine!
DISPATCH
CRACK
CRACK
?? !
I'll take care of your taxis! But before that...
DISPATCH
POW
CRASH
Voilà! That way, you won't escape...!
49

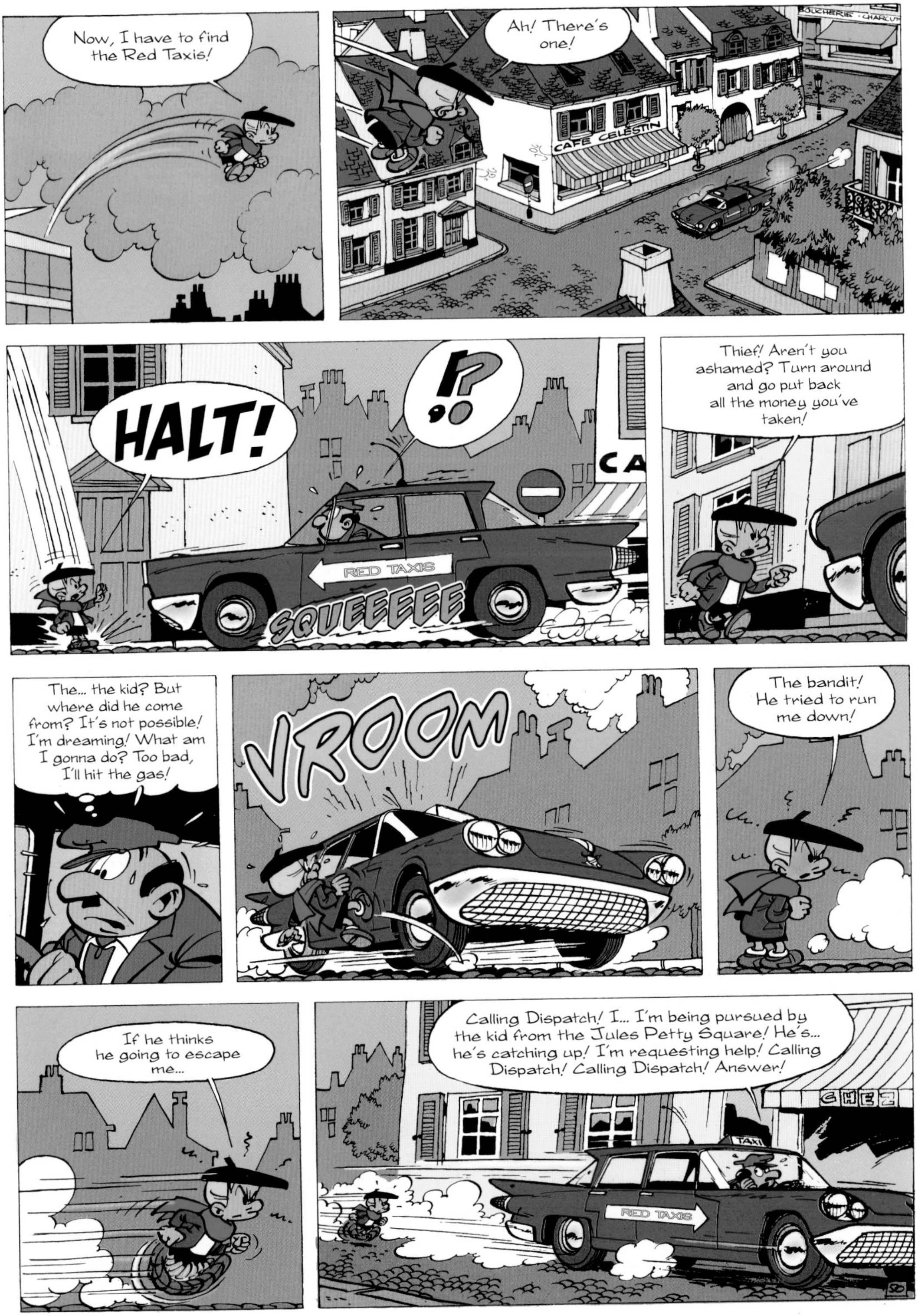
Now, I have to find the Red Taxis!
Ah! There's one!
BOUCHERIE - CHARCUT
CAFE CELESTIN
HALT!
!?
RED TAXIS
SQUEEEEEE
CA
Thief! Aren't you ashamed? Turn around and go put back all the money you've taken!
The... the kid? But where did he come from? It's not possible! I'm dreaming! What am I gonna do? Too bad, I'll hit the gas!
VROOM
The bandit! He tried to run me down!
If he thinks he going to escape me...
Calling Dispatch! I... I'm being pursued by the kid from the Jules Petty Square! He's... he's catching up! I'm requesting help! Calling Dispatch! Calling Dispatch! Answer!
CHEZ
TAXI
RED TAXIS

EH?!

HELP!

What now, eh?
What now?

SMASH

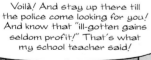
Voilà! And stay up there till the police come looking for you! And know that "ill-gotten gains seldom profit!" That's what my school teacher said!

Good! That's one down! Now for the others!

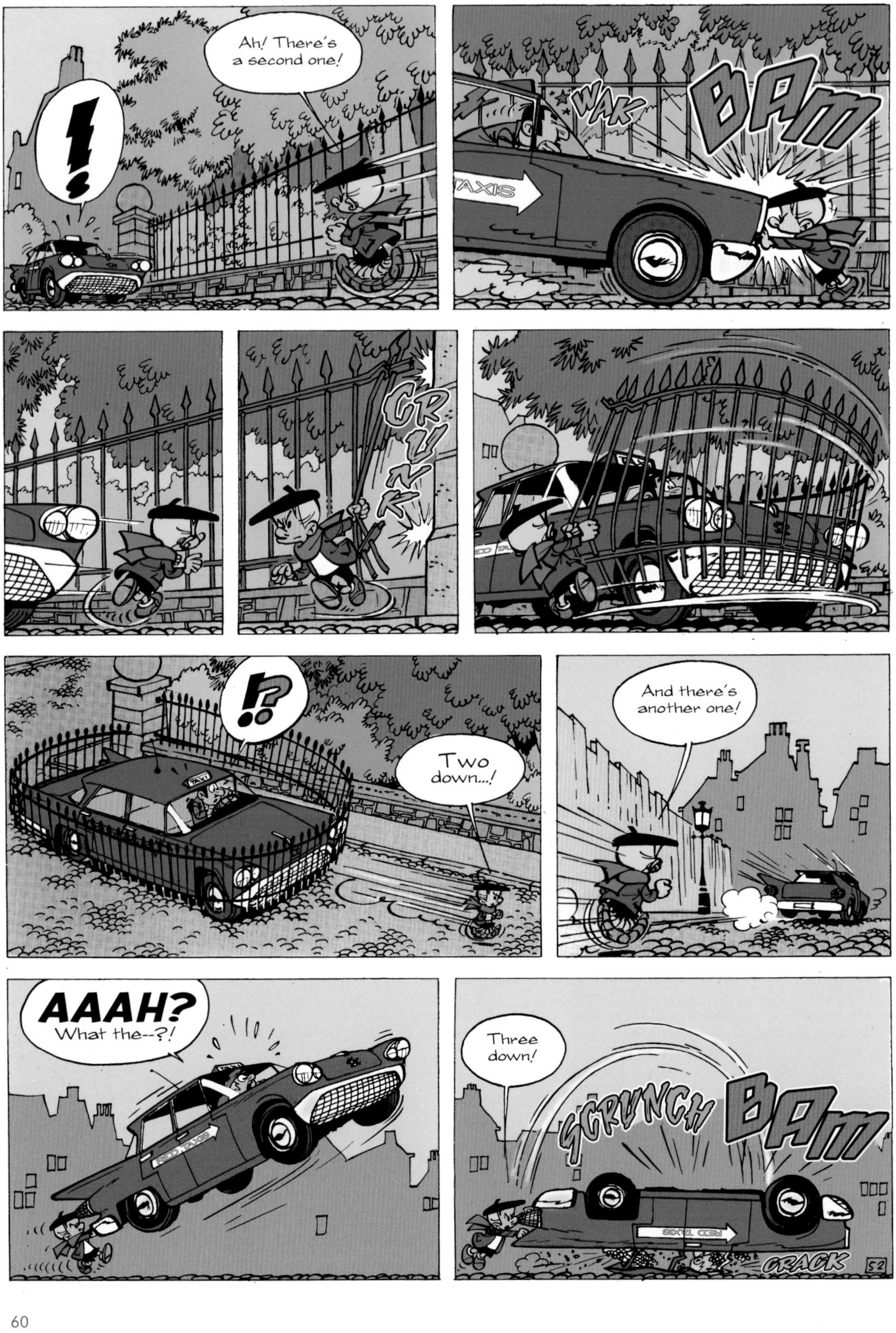
!?
Ah! There's a second one!
WAK
BAM
CRUNK
!?
Two down...!
And there's another one!
AAAH?
What the--?!
Three down!
SCRUNCH
BAM
CRACK
52

Meanwhile, a few miles away...

WHAT?! There never was a radioactive cloud...? But...

...But... however... we saw a... ah? A prank? You think? Uh... yes... thanks!

Little Benny was right! Quick! Let's return to Vivejoie-la-Grande!

And in the meantime...

And if someone took your money, what would you say, eh? Eh...?

C... Calling Dispatch! HELP!

BAM BAM BAM

Faster! FASTER!

Good! There are no Red Taxis left!

Ah! There's the police car! It's arriving just in time!

This time, the police chief will have to recognize that the Red Taxis really were bad guys!

And voilà! The rest is police business! I'm going home!

DAILY NEWS

AN AUDACIOUS HOLD-UP FAILS IN VIVEJOIE-LA-GRANDE

THE WHOLE GANG IS BEHIND BARS

A. HAIRYNOSE, HEAD OF THE RED TAXI COMPANY, WAS, IN FACT, THE HEAD OF A GANG OF CRIMINALS

Mysterious Arrest

Tuesday, at day's end, the population of Vivejoie-la-Grande experienced a panic. Around 5:00 p.m., a violent explosion sounded, soon followed by widespread blackout. A few moments later, the mayor received official notification that a radioactive cloud was heading towards the city. Indeed, at the very moment, a red cloud... immediately, the service for ...entration of

There's a mystery in this whole affair. Indeed, upon returning to Vivejoie-la-Grande, the police found the Red Taxis immobilized or destroyed. One of them was stuck on a tree. And dangling ...by a violent wind had ...ong the

declared being attacked by a small boy having extraordinary strength and who destroyed their cars. Obviously, we cannot give any credence to this incredible tale, and it seems that the criminals invented all this with the goal of being able to plead insanity. Nevertheless, the police say ...concrete explananation ...they saw

A. Hairynose, leaving office of police chief to be led in handcu... the state prison o...

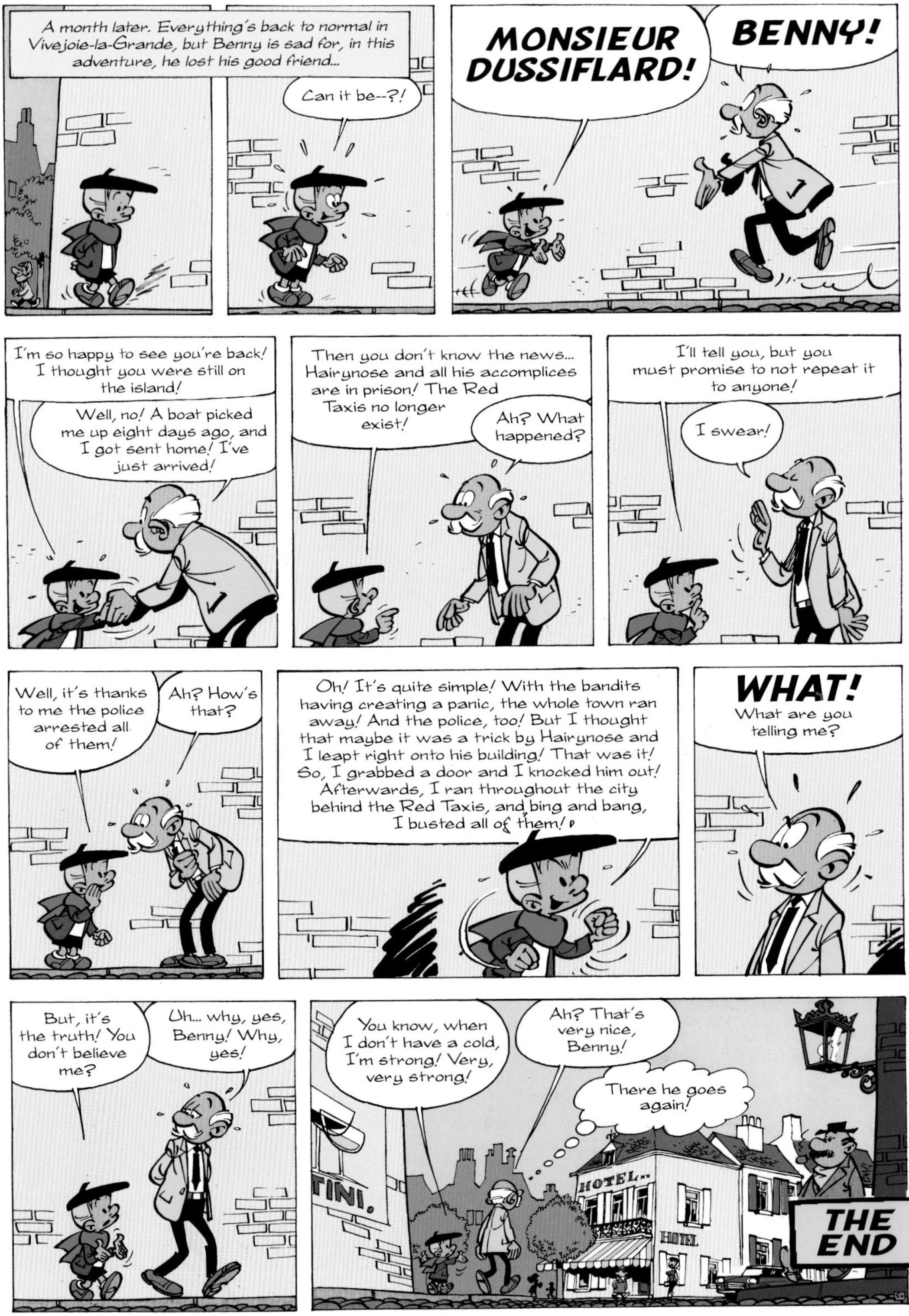

A month later. Everything's back to normal in Vivejoie-la-Grande, but Benny is sad for, in this adventure, he lost his good friend...
Can it be--?!
MONSIEUR DUSSIFLARD!
BENNY!
I'm so happy to see you're back! I thought you were still on the island!
Well, no! A boat picked me up eight days ago, and I got sent home! I've just arrived!
Then you don't know the news... Hairynose and all his accomplices are in prison! The Red Taxis no longer exist!
Ah? What happened?
I'll tell you, but you must promise to not repeat it to anyone!
I swear!
Well, it's thanks to me the police arrested all of them!
Ah? How's that?
Oh! It's quite simple! With the bandits having creating a panic, the whole town ran away! And the police, too! But I thought that maybe it was a trick by Hairynose and I leapt right onto his building! That was it! So, I grabbed a door and I knocked him out! Afterwards, I ran throughout the city behind the Red Taxis, and bing and bang, I busted all of them!
WHAT! What are you telling me?
But, it's the truth! You don't believe me?
Uh... why, yes, Benny! Why, yes!
You know, when I don't have a cold, I'm strong! Very, very strong!
Ah? That's very nice, Benny!
There he goes again!
TINI.
HOTEL
HOTEL
THE END

WATCH OUT FOR PAPERCUTZ™

Welcome to the fast-paced, fun-filled, first BENNY BREAKIRON graphic novel by Peyo from Papercutz, the tough little company dedicated to publishing great graphic novels for all ages. I'm Jim Salicrup, the Editor-in-Chief that has been taking way too many taxis home from work lately.

But seriously, I can't tell you how proud we are at Papercutz to publish another series of graphic novels by Peyo. Many folks in North America may have first encountered Peyo's most famous creation as either an animated TV series or a motion picture, so they may not realize that The Smurfs started as comics in Belgium over fifty years ago. Even fewer may have ever heard of BENNY BREAKIRON, which first appeared in 1962. So maybe now would be the perfect time to find out a bit more about...

Peyo — CREATOR, WRITER, AND ARTIST

Pierre Culliford, born in Belgium June 25, 1928, was a cartoonist known as Peyo. After Peyo left school in Brussels, he looked in the paper for a job. Two caught his eye: offers for a dental assistant and an illustrator. When he presented himself to the dentist, he was told he was just 15 minutes too late! At the time, Belgium was a hothouse of comic strip artists. Peyo quickly found himself working with some of the most talented, amongst them characters such as his lifelong writing partner, Yvan Delporte.

After struggling for some time, he eventually got the break he deserved when he started working for *Le Journal de Spirou*. *Johan and Peewit* were amongst his most popular characters. But in 1958, The Smurfs made their first appearance and went on to become the world-famous characters we now know.

We'll talk more about Peyo and BENNY BREAKIRON next time, in BENNY BREAKIRON #2 "Madame Adolfine." Until then...

Smurfcelsior, Blue-Believers!

Jim

WELCOME TO THE WORLD

BABY SMURF

BORN *February 29th*

WEIGHT *4 Ounces*

LENGTH *2 Inches*

Smurfy wishes from Papa Smurf

AVAILABLE AT BOOKSELLERS EVERWHERE.

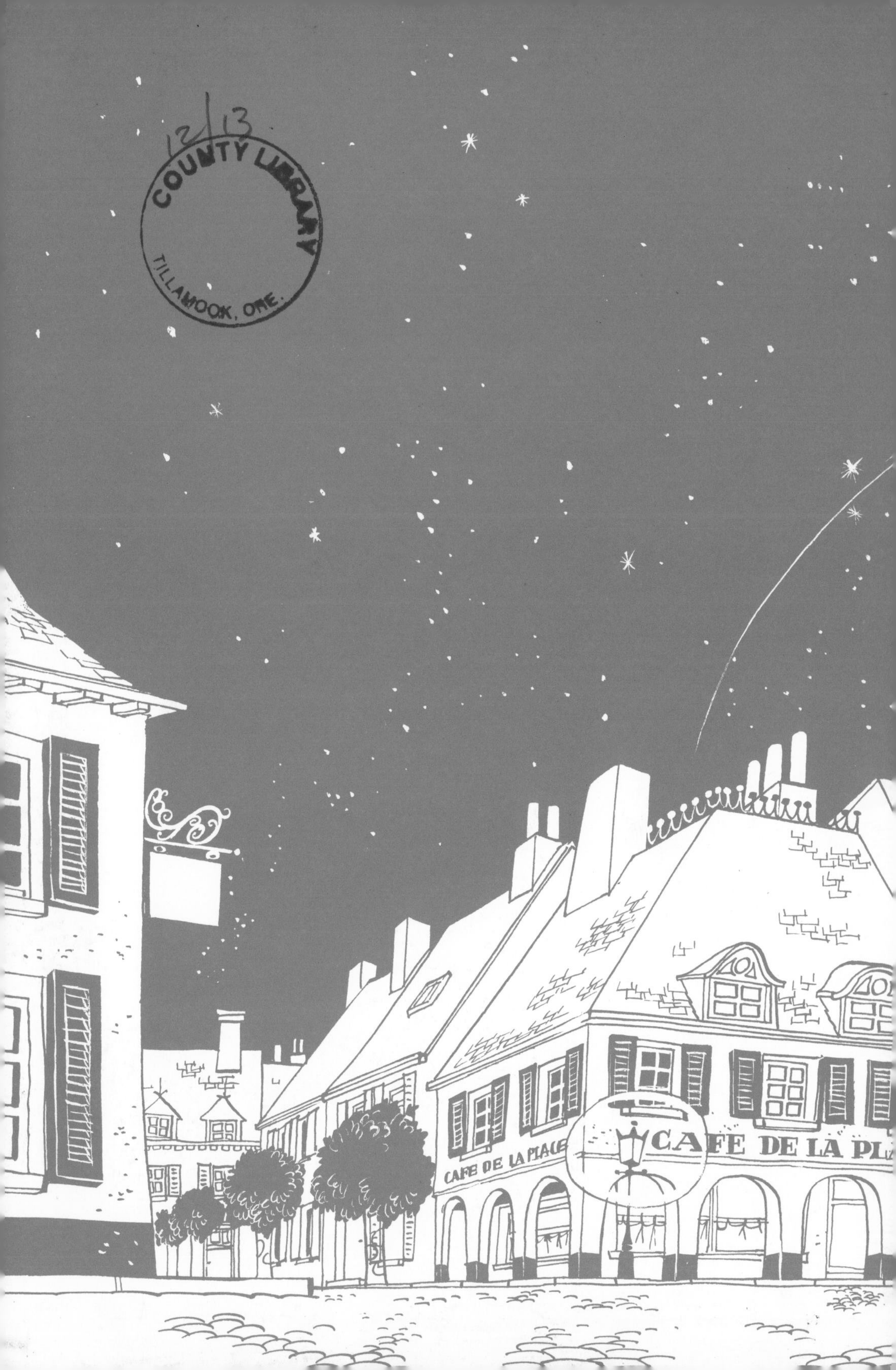
CAFE DE LA PLACE
CAFE DE LA PL